# YOU *Can't* BUY LOVE

## A LIFE LESSONS NOVEL

### BY MELANIE A. SMITH

WICKED DREAMS PUBLISHING

# TABLE OF CONTENTS

# CHAPTER 1

"Do you think it's too soon to propose?"

I stop scanning the crowd of graduates in their caps and gowns waiting for the ceremony to start and slowly turn toward Cal. When his blue eyes meet mine, I can't tell if he's joking or not. He's British, so he always has a small, polite smile on his stupidly handsome face.

"Yes," I say bluntly. I shake my head slightly in annoyance and sigh.

He looks forward again, pensively staring at the stage for a moment, until he says, "I meant, is it too soon for me to propose marriage to Sasha, just to be clear."

I snort. "I knew exactly what you meant," I assure him. "So I presume that was British for, 'But why is it too soon, Jules?'"

Cal presses his lips together, trying to suppress the smile that says that's precisely what he wanted to say.

"Well, now you mention it …" he replies.

"Where do I even begin?" I murmur, more to myself than him. "For starters, Sasha is graduating with her master's in nursing today. And I *know* you wouldn't want to take the attention off that achievement. So today is out."

"I didn't mean —"

I hold up a hand to stop him, which is immensely satisfying as it's something I could never do while we're at work together. He is still more or less one of my supervisors, after all.

"Oh, I'm just getting started," I respond. "Now that she qualifies to become a nurse practitioner, she's going to have to deal with hospital administration to get promoted. And I think we both know *that's* not going to be a walk in the park, even without being engaged to one of the doctors in our unit."

His brows pull together, and he runs a hand through his thick, dark hair. "I hadn't thought about that," he allows.

I raise an eyebrow at his uncharacteristic lack of forethought. "So I presume this idea just popped into your head then?" I ask. "Though you've only been dating, what, four months? Which, by the way, is pretty much why yes, it's way too soon."

Cal blushes, and I have to chuckle. For being a doctor and such a firm presence at Rutherford Hospital since he started five months ago, you'd think he'd be a little smarter about keeping his relationship with one of his nurses under wraps, even if it's not technically against the rules. Not asking his head nurse practitioner, while in a public place mind you, if he should propose.

"You're right," he agrees. "It was a silly idea."

I lay a hand gently on his arm. "Sasha is like family to me," I remind him. "So really, all I care about is whether you really understand what proposing means. If you're ready to stick with her. You know, till death do you part and all. Because if you hurt her, I don't care if you're pretty much one of my bosses, I will have to kill you."

He looks me seriously in the eye. "She's it, Jules. I promise."

My heart melts. I resist reassuring him that they're clearly meant to be and that I know Sasha feels the same way. Because she hasn't outright said it, but we've worked together and been close friends for the better part of a decade. I can just tell.

"Then you have my blessing," I reply.

"To do what?"

I jump in surprise at the voice suddenly coming from my other side. I whirl to see Becca, grinning like she knows exactly how much she just scared the crap out of me.

"About time you showed up," I chastise her, ignoring her question and gesturing to the stage, where an older man in black robes is standing at the podium and tapping the microphone. "They're just about to start."

Becca flips her mane of chocolate curls over her shoulder, hands on hips. All sass, as usual.

"The party never starts without me," she says with a wink, sinking into the chair next to me. As she takes her seat, I notice for the first time her boyfriend is with her. Great, I'm literally surrounded by happy couples.

Not that I don't like Vincent. Becca is as volatile as Sasha is steady. I couldn't have two more different best friends, yet somehow they've both found men who suit them perfectly. Vincent is laid-back enough to deal with Becca's outrageous personality, but still exudes a strength that she bows to. It's actually fascinating to watch, because lord knows as her supervisor I could use a few tips on how to keep her in line.

As the ceremony begins and the speeches drone on, watching Cal watch for Sasha while Becca and Vincent make googly-eyes at each other makes me wonder if I'll ever find someone who suits me perfectly. But it was all I could do to get time off on a Saturday to make it to a huge milestone in one of my closest friend's lives. Anything besides that or someone dying, and there's no way I'd be able to get away from work. That all of us somehow managed it is nothing short of a miracle. Anyway, with that kind of schedule, dating is pretty much off the table.

I shouldn't complain. I do love my job, despite recent struggles with the way the hospital is run that have made it less enjoyable than it once was. Though understaffed hospitals and overworked medical professionals aren't exactly uncommon. And this life was my choice.

That's my mantra: This choice was mine. There are a lot of things you can't control with any job. But I get to help people, get them out of pain, out of fear, and hopefully living better lives.

It's why I asked to be in the cardiac unit over emergency, intensive care, or even maternity. I've worked all over the hospital, and cardiac is one of the few units where you often see the same patients regularly, get to know them, and get to really understand your impact on their lives.

Bringing myself back to the moment, I watch Sasha take the stage finally to accept her diploma. Her dark blond hair is pulled into a conservative ponytail, her grin wide and infectious as her eyes nervously scan the crowd, probably searching for Cal. It occurs to me that my closest friends, who started as just coworkers, have impacted *my* life just as much as we impact our patients'. How would I make it through each day without these strong, supportive women? Let's be honest — I probably wouldn't.

So, while I'm happy that they're both coming into full lives of career success, love, and all that … well, I can't help noticing that I'm standing still. Possibly even going backward as the jerks in charge of my job continue to test the limits of my patience and hamper my ability to give the best care possible. I can feel it changing me, tearing at the shreds of my sanity.

I shake myself, focusing back on the moment once more as the ceremony wraps up and we rise to find Sasha and shower her with the love and pride she deserves.

* * *

When I get back to my small, quiet apartment that night, I settle onto the still practically brand-new couch. Even though I've had it for years, I'm not exactly here enough to lounge around on it. I mostly stumble home after a workday that's twelve hours at best, sometimes stretching to as many as sixteen, after which I bolt down dinner — assuming cheese and deli meat on crackers with half a bottle of wine counts as a meal — then fall asleep fully clothed on top of my bed with the TV on in the background.

It's a glamorous life I lead. Thankfully, this evening I'm spared my usual crap dinner, as we'd all gone out after the ceremony for a real meal. But without the physical exertion I'd have had throughout the day at work, my relatively calm outing has left me wide awake. And with far too much time to think. A dangerous situation for a single thirty-four-year-old woman who is becoming increasingly unhappy with her career, her love life — or lack thereof — and ... well, life in general. I haven't even had time to admit that to myself until this moment.

I rise restlessly, stalking into the bathroom. A long, hot shower can fix just about anything. I turn on the tap and examine my face in the mirror as the water heats. My dark red hair is getting ridiculously long, trailing almost down to my backside. Which is saying something, given that I'm five-foot-ten. My naturally thin frame is leaning toward undernourished from long hours, hard work, and little food. I've never been one to remember to eat regularly, and it's taking its toll. The dark circles under my eyes, despite my attempts at hiding them with makeup, pretty much underscore that I'm desperately in need of more than five or six hours of sleep a night, some downtime, and probably a whole lot of other crap that falls under "self-care." As a medical professional, you'd think I'd take my own advice and look after my health. But I've always been better at helping others do that.

I turn my back on my reflection and get in the shower. The heat instantly soothes me, and I stand under the scalding stream until I physically can't take it anymore.

Once I'm out and dried off, I don't even dress, simply flopping down on the bed in my robe. Life finally catches up with me, and my mind goes blissfully blank as I drift to sleep.

* * *

"Sundays are for rest and fun, Jules. You don't have to come in here *every* week on your only day off," Katie scolds me as I tidy the common area of my parents' nursing home.

"Don't start," I warn her. "You know I'd come in to see Mom and Dad anyway."

Katie's big brown eyes give me a pitying look, and she doesn't even have to say it. I know they don't recognize me, but it doesn't matter. They're still my parents, and it comforts me to see them, to be part of their lives, even if it doesn't change anything.

I avoid talking about it, continuing to fold blankets, arrange magazines, or whatever the hell else will keep my hands and mind busy.

"You seem especially restless today," she remarks.

"Is there anything you don't notice?" I turn to her and cross my arms over my chest.

She gives me a patient smile. "We've been friends a long time," she reminds me. "Are things at the hospital that bad? Or is it something else?"

I watch my parents at the table in the corner while I consider how to answer her question. It still amazes me how, even though they don't know each other, much less their own daughter, they still somehow always need to be in each other's spheres. My heart aches at the thought of a love so deep that, on some level, it persists even through the ravages of their respective diseases.

"You know the Rutherford Group," I murmur distractedly. In fact, Katie was a nurse at my hospital before going into elderly care. It's how we met, all those years ago. "Always focused on expansion. It's just been an annoyance in the past as far as funding goes, but it's changed things too much now. Taken too much from the hospital. I just don't get why they don't care more about that."

"Maybe they don't know?" Katie suggests, continuing to count pills to go with the lunches we'll serve shortly.

I look up and catch her eye. "I know what you're trying to say, and there's no way in hell I'm going around my bosses to tell them. I'm already in enough trouble with MacDougall for speaking my mind at last quarter's budget meeting as it is."

"Suit yourself," she replies.

Damn Katie and her gentle nudges. She's right, really. Someone needs to say something.

"So what happens to Mom and Dad," I say, my voice thick with emotion as I gesture angrily at my parents, "when I lose my job for fighting that battle? Who's going to pay for their care?"

Katie looks up evenly at me. "Now, Jules, it's not me you're really mad at, is it?"

I snort. Katie is almost like a mother to me, and it's hard not to resent her honesty sometimes. Especially when I'm not ready to hear it, much less do something about it.

"No, I'm not," I finally agree.

"So who? Dr. MacDougall is the chief of cardiac. As self-important as he's always been, he's just a puppet of hospital administration. You know that," she chides.

"I know," I admit. "Unfortunately, he's as far up the food chain as I'm allowed to go without endangering my job. But believe me, I've been tempted to drive straight to Warren Rutherford's office and give him a piece of my mind."

Katie's eyebrows jump. "Surely, you realize that going directly to the president and CEO of the Rutherford Group is overkill. There must be someone between Malcolm MacDougall and Warren Rutherford who can do something."

I shrug. "If I'm going to risk my ass, might as well go straight to the top. Besides, it's his name on the fucking hospital. He should know what kind of reputation he really has among people who aren't paid to kiss his ass."

She laughs. "Except you are paid to kiss his ass, indirectly, as it were," she points out.

I shake my head. "Oh, Katie, you know me better than that. I grew up with nothing. Money means shit to me. There's no amount of it you could pay me to kiss anyone's ass, *especially* not Warren Rutherford."

Her aged lips pucker. "You're lucky everyone here but me is senile and won't repeat that to anyone who matters.

Be careful, okay? We can always figure out a way to take care of your parents, but I'd hate to see you tank your career."

"It's all talk," I assure her. "You know I'm only blowing off steam. I'll keep going, same as I always have. Taking it up the ass with a smile on my face."

Katie gives me a mischievous smile. "You say that like taking it up the ass is —"

I throw my hands over my ears. "Gah! Don't even go there," I say, squeezing my eyes shut. "My fault, I should know better than to say things like that around you."

Mother figure or not, Katie has always been *way* too comfortable talking about sex. Had she worked at Rutherford at the same time as Becca, I imagine they'd have been thick as thieves. And I'm no shrinking violet but, in my opinion, some things should stay private.

I peel open an eye to see that Katie has walked off, chuckling to herself. I shake my head and walk to the kitchen to start on lunch. As much as I hate talking about Rutherford, budgets, and their fucked-up politics, I'm just glad Katie didn't get on me about dating again. I've got enough crap to worry about without the pressure to add a man to the mix. Lord knows they usually cause more problems than they solve.

# CHAPTER 2

"Damn, Sash, back at work at six a.m. on a Monday morning already. Isn't there, like, a honeymoon for graduates?" Becca asks, tapping her chin thoughtfully.

Sasha rolls her eyes as she puts her purse in a drawer, and my eyes shoot sharply to Becca, wondering if Cal said something to her about proposing too. I sure hope not. He, of all people, should know what a gossip she is and that his chances of keeping it under wraps would be zero once she knew. I may be tied into the gossip loop to keep tabs, but Becca nearly lives for it.

Thankfully, Becca doesn't return my look, so I'm fairly certain it was just an offhand comment.

"Honestly, Becks, if there were, do you really think I'd take one anyway?" Sasha shoots back.

"True story, my too-serious sister-from-another-mister," Becca replies with a wink.

"God, you're all perky again now that you're getting laid regularly," Sasha grumbles.

The three of us snap to attention as Cal turns the corner.

"Good morning, Dr. Thompson," we say in unison.

"Good morning, ladies," he replies, winking at us as he passes. Well, probably winking at Sasha. But I'll take it. It's the most male attention I'm bound to get this week, save elderly patients who can't keep their wrinkled paws to themselves. Though that's lessened since Cal joined and helped put a stop to the backlash for reporting those kinds of things.

A lot has changed since he started working here, really. Aside from curbing patient sexual harassment toward the staff, he's also convinced hospital administration to upgrade a few key pieces of medical equipment that were hopelessly ancient technology. Unfortunately, it was only a few, and we're still drastically behind across the board. And the expenditures made us even shorter on funds for staffing. Two steps forward, ten steps back.

"All right, ladies, time for the morning staff meeting," I say, throwing as much pep into my words as I can.

"Oh, boy," Becca grumbles sarcastically as she rises to join me.

I ignore her and march us into the conference room. MacDougall trails in behind us, clearing his voice pointedly to quiet the assembled crowd.

He goes through his usual lectures before reminding us that this Thursday is the Rutherford Group's annual charity event and that anyone who wants to attend can coordinate to have their shifts covered if necessary. It takes everything I have not to snort disdainfully.

Seriously, it's just an excuse for San Diego's elite to suck up to one another, schmooze, and have free booze, all in the name of whatever pet cause they've picked this time around. Nobody but the chiefs and directors ever attend. Why would we? We're the little people, we mean nothing to them. They'd probably mistake us for the serving staff or something anyway.

Finally, the meeting is over, and we can actually start getting real work done. Except, as I go to leave, MacDougall catches my arm.

"Ms. Magnusson, I'd like a word," he says quietly.

I suppress an eyeroll. Even when he was just another doctor, MacDougall always called me "Ms. Magnusson." Not "Nurse Magnusson" or "Julianna" like all the other doctors do. Just another way he's always treated me differently. I swear, the old bastard has it out for me.

"What can I do for you, Dr. MacDougall?" I ask as pleasantly as I possibly can.

"I'm afraid my wife is having surgery this Thursday and I'll need to be available to her that evening. I'd like you to go to the gala in my stead."

My jaw drops. "Surely one of the doctors should cover instead?" I ask, already knowing he'll consider that "talking back."

"Given your recent criticisms of leadership, I think it would be a good opportunity for you to observe their capacity for generosity," he says. "And the importance of our role in the greater cause for advancing medicine."

I fight to keep the sneer off my face. As if whatever fakery was put on at this fancy party would stop me from remembering all the ways in which our "leadership" is screwing us right now. No, that's not what this is. He knows how much I hate this kind of bullshit. This isn't an opportunity. It's punishment for embarrassing him in front of the budget committee, plain and simple. I take a slow, deep breath and remind myself: You chose this job. You can deal with these assholes for one night.

"Well, sir, I suppose if you think I'm the best person to represent our department, then I'd be delighted," I reply sweetly.

He quirks an eyebrow. "Excellent," he says. "See that you stay the whole evening and do try to make a good impression on behalf of the staff here. I'll arrange for your shift on Friday to be covered accordingly. And, Ms. Magnusson?" I raise an eyebrow to acknowledge him. "I expect you to show all of our administrators the respect they're due, as well as Mr. Rutherford and his guests."

Now both my eyebrows shoot up. Warren Rutherford will actually be there. I guess I hadn't thought about that part. Well, this presents a potential opportunity, indeed. A very risky opportunity. But still, one to consider. And hey, either way, I get Friday off. I can't remember the last time that happened.

"Of course," I agree curtly.

With a contemplative look, MacDougall nods and takes his leave. And all I can think is, *Oh, I'll show them the respect they're due, all right.*

* * *

"I can't wear that," I scoff as Becca holds up the daring red dress. The thick silk, strapless mermaid-style gown has an extreme sweetheart neckline and is far more overtly sexy than anything I've ever worn. That's not even my main objection, though. Red? With my hair? She's nuts.

"Trust me," she insists. I give her a deeply skeptical look, at which she rolls her eyes and thrusts the dress in my direction. "At least try it on."

I grimace but take it from her and lay it over the dresses I'd selected. And, not for the first or last time, I wish Sasha didn't have to work late tonight. I have no doubt she'd help me pick a dress I was actually comfortable in.

Just to needle Becca, I try on a conservative cream-colored ballgown first. As I stand in the changing room, I have to admit I'm not that excited by it. But it definitely screams "rich and snobby," so I figure it's probably appropriate. I open the door and step into the wide seating area, complete with pedestal and three-paneled mirror.

Becca's face instantly sours. "You look like a fuddy-duddy," she says.

I laugh. "That's kind of the point. Blend in with all the other fuddy-duddies."

She shakes her head and pushes me up on the pedestal so I can fully appreciate the disaster that is this dress.

"You look shapeless. And boring. You're gorgeous, Jules. Why would you want to hide that under all this damn fabric?"

I roll my eyes. "Fine, I agree, this dress sucks. I'll go try on the other one I picked."

"Nonononono," she objects, wagging a finger at me. "Red dress next."

"Fine, whatever gets this done fastest," I agree, lifting the giant skirt. I still almost trip getting off the platform. If it wasn't already out, it would be now. I can totally see myself falling down a set of stairs in this behemoth.

Once back in the dressing room, I shed the dress, unceremoniously piling it in the corner, then I slip into the red dress.

Before I even look in the mirror, the soft fabric against my skin feels like heaven. A rich person's heaven. It's beyond luxurious feeling. So when I turn toward the mirror, I'm already a little sad knowing it's going to look horrible against my auburn locks.

Except it doesn't. The bright red somehow perfectly compliments my hair color *and* skin tone. And holy hell, is it sexy. The plunging sweetheart neckline fits perfectly around my chest, shaping me in a way that puts the girls where they used to be ten years ago. It's a lot of cleavage, but I've never felt more beautiful. I open the door, now expecting the fabric that's fitted snugly against my outer thighs and knees to make walking practically impossible.

Except it doesn't. It has just enough give to make walking feel like being caressed every time I take a step.

My eyes are wide when Becca notices me. She jumps up, clapping her hands.

"Yasss, girl," she calls. "Damn, you look hot."

She grabs me, practically shoving me up onto the platform. She fusses around me, flaring the base of the dress. Then, she wrangles a salesperson to get some shoes that match, so we can get the full effect.

I'm silent as she works, carefully smoothing my hair over my shoulder so it cascades down one side in the front. I dip my head forward so it falls over my eye, giving myself a sultry look. Somehow my hazel eyes look greener now. I seriously look like a model in a fashion magazine. This dress is miraculous.

Becca catches my eye in the mirror, smirking.

"See. Told you. Tell me you don't love this dress."

"I don't love this dress," I deadpan.

She pulls a skeptical face.

"I want to *live in it*," I breathe, doing an impatient little dance.

"Girl, if I looked like that in something, I'd want to live in it too," she responds. "Just promise me you'll at least use this dress to get a little ass."

My mouth pops open. "Becca!" I gasp.

"What? You can't tell me it hasn't been a long time. And if you can't get some looking like *that*, well ..." She shrugs.

I roll my eyes. "As if I'd be interested in any of the billionaire playboys who will be there. They're witless morons with too much money, too few manners, and a yen for a photo-op so they can show off the fact that they can give away millions left and right. Please."

"Fine, then a cute waiter or something. I'm just sayin', you never know," she says. "But you are getting this dress, yes?"

I take a deep breath and look at my reflection. "Yes," I sigh.

Becca grins. "That's my girl," she says with a wink. "And if nothing else, you can knock Warren Rutherford dead before, you know, ripping him a new one."

That gets a laugh out of me. "Eh. I'll only be ripping him a new one in my dreams. But I like where your head's at," I reply.

"We'll see," she murmurs. "Personally, I can't think of anyone better to put the old bastard in his place. He'll never know what hit him."

As I stare at myself in the mirror, I think about that. This dress makes me feel bold, that's for sure. Let's just hope it doesn't encourage me to do anything stupid.

# CHAPTER 3

"I'm sorry, can you repeat that?" I ask, stopping in my tracks. So abruptly, apparently, that Sasha keeps walking a few steps before she realizes I'm no longer next to her.

She turns back to me, stepping close so she can keep her voice down. "They said I can have the job but not the promotion," she repeats.

My brows scrunch together. "What does that mean?" I ask. But almost as soon as the words are out of my mouth, it clicks into place. They want Sasha to do all the work without the title or pay. I gasp at their audacity. "*No.* They wouldn't."

"Would and did," she grumbles. "I don't know what to do, Jules. They're hiring NPs right now at UCSD Medical for nearly twenty thousand more a year than I'm making."

I shake my head slowly. "This is insane. They know we need another ARNP in the unit. Sarah and I are working ourselves to death trying to cover everything."

She shrugs sadly. "Clearly, they're happy to let you keep doing that. Or let me get away if I don't like their offer."

My eyes meet hers. "You're not really thinking of leaving, are you?" I ask. But then I feel like a selfish ass. "Of course you are, I'm sorry. I understand. You need to do what's best for you. But my god, how can they do this to you after all your years here?"

"Things have changed here," Sasha points out. "To be honest, between the way things are now and being with Cal, it might be for the best if I leave anyway."

"I thought you loved it here?" I can't help trying to convince her to stay. It'd be like losing a family member if she left. Even though I know we'd still see each other outside of work. It would just be one more thing that made this place less bearable.

"In some ways, I do," she agrees. "But come on, Jules. I know neither of us are the type to complain, but ..." She looks around to make sure nobody is listening, then lowers her voice. "Shit's bad."

I have to laugh at that. "True."

Unfortunately, I have an appointment, so we part ways, unable to talk more about it. But the whole thing just sits poorly with me all morning.

So, after lunch, I do something I know is probably stupid and go see MacDougall in his office. It goes about as well as I expect, and it's a complete waste of breath to attempt to convince him that we *need* another official nurse practitioner for scheduling reasons, that Sasha has invested eight years at Rutherford and deserves it, that they're going to lose her if they don't step up. It's all for naught, and we're both annoyed with each other by the time I leave his office nearly an hour later.

When I leave that afternoon, early so I can get ready for the gala, I'm not so convinced I'll be able to keep my mouth shut if I run into Warren Rutherford. Or, you know, if I seek him out for the sole purpose of letting him know exactly what I think of his expansion strategy and its impacts on the hospital that started it all. Because if Sasha goes ... well, it's the first proverbial rat fleeing the sinking ship. And maybe I should take the hint.

# YOU CAN'T BUY LOVE

*  *  *

Dressed to the nines with a pair of slender silver heels and a black clutch to complement the stunning gown Becca chose, my hair is sleek and curled, my makeup dramatic and sexy. I've never felt so confident.

But, in the back of the Uber I called to take me to the gala, I also decide that tonight isn't the time or place to make my stand. I just need to endure this punishment and not get myself in any more trouble. Mouthing off isn't going to help. I doubt I'll be able to get anywhere near Warren Rutherford anyway, though even if I could, why would he listen? He wouldn't. So no point in risking my job for nothing.

When I arrive at the swanky marina-front hotel around seven, it's still fully light out and pleasantly warm. Thankfully, the strapless, figure-hugging dress also seems to breathe well, because I feel cool and dry under its silky fabric.

I rearrange my hair back over one shoulder so it cascades down my front. I stare up at the impressive awning over the hotel's entrance, including giant, domed chandeliers already lighting the expensively tiled pathway. I roll my eyes at the opulence as well-dressed people stream by me, getting it out of my system.

With a resigned sigh, I make my way inside to be greeted by a stunning glass- and wood-paneled wall. Six huge panels tile across the center, a gorgeous fragmented purple and blue wave cresting across its width. I don't realize I'm blocking traffic with my gawking until I'm elbowed sharply, waking me up to the fact that I'm standing in the middle of the entrance.

With a deep blush, I watch those in formal wear splitting off to the sides and disappearing into archways on either side of the hotel's front desk. As I follow, I note signs directing attendees of the Rutherford Group's annual gala to the Grand Hall. I descend stairs under one of the archways, and the first thing I notice is huge, dark, wood-paneled doors that open into a gigantic ballroom in front of me. I'm too busy trying to take everything in to notice the podiums on either side of the ballroom entrance.

"Name on your ticket, ma'am?" the attendant at the podium to my right asks. I look over to see a woman in a navy hotel uniform smiling politely at me.

I feel myself blush again as I backtrack a step or two.

"I'm so sorry. It's Julianna Magnusson," I offer. "I'm attending in Dr. Malcom MacDougall's place."

A few taps on a tablet later, and she offers me a plastic square something like a credit card, with a number printed on it and a chip embedded in the corner.

"Here you are, Ms. Magnusson," she says. "You may use this to bid on any of the silent auction items inside. Cocktails are being served here and also in the Seaport Foyer upstairs. You'll use your card to attend the banquet in the Seaport Ballroom in an hour and to be admitted to the concert in the Harbor Ballroom, also on the second floor, later this evening."

My eyebrows shoot up as I thank her and take the card, slipping it into my clutch. This whole affair is even fancier than I thought. It must've cost a fortune. But then, judging by the fat cats happily crowding the auction items lined on tables against the walls, I imagine it's going to pay off quite nicely. Plenty of other partygoers gather at small, standing-only tables scattered around the center of the room as waiters with trays of drinks and appetizers make their rounds.

As I move forward I notice that just past the entrance, in the center of the room, is a large sign on a golden stand declaring that all proceeds from the evening will go to the Alzheimer's Foundation of America. All the air goes out of my lungs and my eyes fill with tears. I know MacDougall couldn't have known that that's what slowly took my father from me over the past decade, but it makes me hate him all the more. How can I watch these people, who can buy the best of everything, including medical care, have a party under the guise of helping people like my father, who were helpless physically and financially against the ravages of this disease?

I know I should be happy that they're raising money for Alzheimer's research. But looking around at the people laughing, drinking, and socializing, it all feels so wrong. This. This is why I never come to these things. Do any of these people really even care?

As a waiter with a tray full of tall flutes of sparkling wine passes in front of me, I deftly snatch one and gulp half of it in one go. I know MacDougall said "the whole evening," but if I can manage to at least survive through dinner and speeches, I figure that's enough. You know, in case there's a pop quiz. Though even that could be another two hours or more. Either way, after that I'm out of here. Until then, booze.

I finish my drink and swap my empty for another full glass before I approach one end of the silent auction spread, intending to at least work my way around the room to see what ridiculous, over-the-top prizes are being offered. And I'm not far off. There's the normal stuff like gift baskets of luxury spa products and chocolate, amusement park vacation packages, and service gift cards for photographers, masseurs, and catering. The kinds of things that local businesses pitch in to support a good cause and attract new customers. But there's also a private concert by a big-name pop artist, a week's vacation in a villa in Tuscany including airfare and a private driver and translator, and a private yacht party for up to three hundred people. Yeesh. Rich people. I bet those last ones all come directly from Warren Rutherford and friends.

But when I come across a four-hour sunset hot air balloon ride experience up the coast, I can't help it. I stop, a pang of longing shooting through me. Riding in a hot air balloon has been on my bucket list as long as I can remember. I've looked into it, but even if I could get the time off work, the cheapest one I've found is the better part of a thousand dollars, and I really can't justify that.

I take a deep drink of the champagne in my hand. With a glass and a half of liquid courage bubbling in my veins, and wearing a dress that makes me feel like I can do anything … well, I can't help myself from tapping the small machine next to the description with my card and entering a modest bid. When in Rome and all. And maybe I'll get extra points with MacDougall for actually participating.

"Good choice," says a voice next to me.

I look up, and my head swims a little at the motion from the effects of the alcohol. That's what I get for being a hundred and twenty pounds and downing it so fast on an empty stomach.

But if I thought that was dizzying, it's nothing compared to the man fixing me with the most gorgeous smile I've ever seen. On an equally gorgeous face framed by well-styled medium brown hair, with deep-set light brown eyes that remind me of golden honey. His full lips are parted ever so slightly as his eyes slide down my body, sending shivers up my spine.

"Thanks," I manage as my eyes travel over his well-tailored classic black tux. Even in heels, he's just a bit taller than me, with broad shoulders and a strong build. My tummy flip-flops. I tell myself it's the alcohol. Or I try to tell myself that. But being a little tipsy … well, I don't want to listen.

He extends a hand. "I'm Noah," he offers.

"Julianna," I reply, slipping my hand in his. Instead of shaking it, he raises it to his lips, placing a kiss on the back. And I swear, I've never understood what the word "swoon" really meant in a romantic sense until this moment.

"That's a beautiful name," he replies.

I don't even care how cheesy his line is, every deep, spine-tingling word out of his mouth fans the flames of my attraction to him.

"You can call me Jules," I counter.

He cocks an eyebrow and gives me a devilish smile as he lets go of my hand. "Duly noted. Sorry, I don't have a nickname. It's just Noah." His grin widens.

"It's a good name," I reply with a shy smile. God, I'm such an idiot.

He laughs. "Thanks. So, why the balloon ride?" he asks, gesturing around. "Of all the things on offer."

Another partygoer approaches, forcing me to step aside to let them access the machine. Putting me closer to the handsome and alluring man in front of me.

I look up at him, having to remind myself to breathe. Though that just reinforces his effect on me as I get a whiff of his intoxicating, expensive-smelling cologne. I clear my throat, trying to shake it off.

"I've always wanted to ride in a hot air balloon," I reply with a simple shrug.

"Ah, so you've never been before?"

I shake my head lightly, indicating I haven't. "Plus, you know, it's for a good cause and all."

His expression turns pensive. "Yes, yes it is," he murmurs. He looks up again, catching my eye. "So what do you do, Julianna?"

Hearing him purposefully use my full name sends another set of shivers running through me. Both because he intentionally ignored my direction, and because it sounds *so* good coming out of his mouth.

"I work at Rutherford Hospital," I admit.

He grins so wide, I notice a dimple in his left cheek. Could this man get any hotter?

"Let me guess. You're a nurse," he replies.

I put my hands on my hips. "Why, because I'm a woman?" I shoot back. "I could be a doctor for all you know."

He presses his lips together for a moment, clearly trying to suppress a smile. "No, because I know all the doctors at Rutherford," he explains. "I work for the Rutherford Group in operations. We liaise with hospital administration."

I raise an eyebrow. And I'm briefly tempted to find out if this guy has any pull. But then I remember, I'm playing nice tonight and *not* putting myself in a position to get fired.

"I see," I say shortly.

He studies my face for a moment, and I wonder what he's trying to read there.

"Let's not talk about work," he finally replies, as if he can tell going down that path would lead to nothing good. "Tell me more about *you*."

I take another nervous gulp of champagne, emptying my glass this time. "What would you like to know?"

Noah flags down a waiter and gestures for my glass. I hand it over but wave off a refill. Best to wait until dinner, when I've got something in my stomach to help slow the drunkenness.

"Well, let's start with where you're from. Are you a San Diego native?" he asks, taking a glass of champagne for himself and leading me to one of the tables so we're out of the way.

"Born and bred," I admit. "You?"

"Same," he replies.

He proceeds to question me about everything — age, though not directly, whether I have siblings, my favorite foods, hobbies, those sorts of topics. And I quiz him right back. The more we talk, the less I feel like tonight is punishment. Among other things, I find out he's forty, a never-married and self-professed workaholic, has an older brother and a younger sister, and likes skiing, when he can get away for it. And that every word out of his mouth makes me like him more. But that might be the obvious chemistry floating between us as we share coy looks and smiles. I haven't flirted in so long, it almost feels like it shouldn't come this easily. But then, he's so easy to talk to. And so, so dreamy.

Unfortunately, we're interrupted about twenty minutes later when a nervous-looking young man in his mid-twenties approaches and gets Noah's attention, telling him something discreetly in his ear.

He turns back to me with an apologetic look. "I'm so sorry, but I need to step away to take care of something work related," Noah says.

I can't help my look of surprise. "So much for not talking about work tonight," I tease. "It's fine, though, really. It was lovely chatting with you."

He lifts my hand, placing another kiss on the back. "And I enjoyed chatting with you. I'll look for you later at the banquet, Julianna."

And with a confident wink that sets loose a cadre of butterflies in my stomach, he's gone.

I try not to look like a lost puppy once I'm on my own again. To avoid just that, I decide to find my way upstairs to see if there are more interesting cocktail options in the Seaport Foyer.

I'm not disappointed, on several counts, as not even a few minutes later, a Manhattan in hand, I'm heading onto a beautiful terrace just off the foyer that overlooks the marina. The sun is just starting to sink toward the horizon, and I don't think it's a coincidence that dinner was timed with sunset. It's absolutely stunning, showcasing all the best things about San Diego as the boats dip lazily in water that sparkles with all the colors of the clear sky.

But surprisingly few other partygoers are on the balcony. Not that I mind. It means I get to watching the changing colors above me without pressure, without having to schmooze, all while fulfilling my requirement to be physically present.

At nearly eight, I decide I'll stay to watch the sunset before going in, even if it makes me late. It's just too gorgeous to pass up.

"Beautiful, isn't it?"

Wondering how I already know his voice so well, I turn with a smile to see Noah settling his arms on the balcony next to me.

"How'd you find me?" I ask.

He straightens up and gives my dress an obvious once over. "You're hard to miss."

I let my hair shift into my face. I'm both flattered and a little shy again all of a sudden.

I feel his hand slip under my chin, lifting my face to look up into his.

"You can try to hide behind that gorgeous mane," he says, running his thumb along my jaw, "but red dress or not, you were born to stand out, Julianna."

"We should get inside," I mumble. My eyes dart to the glass doors behind us, to the crowds of people filing into the ballroom. "Dinner is starting."

He considers me for a moment, not moving an inch.

"Meet me after. Right here."

"You're awfully bossy," I remark, my lips curling into a smile despite myself.

"Are you saying you don't want to?" he teases, his hand sliding from my face, down my shoulder, over my arm to hold my hand in his.

I give his hand a small squeeze before withdrawing, frankly overwhelmed by how drawn to this man I am. I'm not used to noticing men or being attracted to them, much less actually wanting to act on it.

"I'm not sure yet," I reply.

He tips his head back and laughs. "Oh, I think you are. But you're not a risk-taker, are you?" His heated gaze is borderline cocky as he watches me. "I'll be here at ten. I hope you are too." But something about his tone is so sure that I can tell he thinks I will be, which is underscored when he doesn't say another word before walking back into the foyer. I lose sight of him quickly as he slips into the crowd.

While I watch the sun fully set, even I don't know what I'll do. Because this second meeting had a different tenor to it. His invitation was laced with the promise of something I haven't allowed myself in a very long time.

Too long, I decide. It's time to make Becca proud. Not that that's the measure by which I live my life. But I've been hardworking, single-minded, and overly cautious for so long. And sometimes it's good to do something you'd never normally do. Or someone, in this case.

With a catlike grin, I turn and head in for dinner.

I scan my card as I enter to receive my seating assignment, and discover I'm sharing a table with the Rutherford Hospital chiefs, all of whom I know rather well. So dinner is a much more comfortable affair than anticipated, especially knowing many of them secretly side with me over MacDougall and aren't really thrilled about being here with the glitterati either.

The food is divine, of course, though I nearly choke on it when the head of maternity jokes that it better be for a thousand dollars a plate. So when the speeches start a few minutes later, I'm already back in a place of appalled disgust at the opulent show of wealth and arrogance that surrounds this whole event.

The first speaker is from the Alzheimer's Foundation, which I actually enjoy. Hearing that this event might actually do some good makes me just slightly less grumpy. But when that's followed by a speech by Warren Rutherford himself, touting the Rutherford Group's stellar reputation, state-of-the-art hospitals, and vast resources that must be used to advance medical solutions and not just fix medical problems … I swear to the Almighty, it takes every ounce of strength I have not to call him out on the spot.

# YOU CAN'T BUY LOVE

I actually even think about what I'll say. But I realize three things: First, being near the entrance of the room, with the stage on the opposite side of the cavernous space, there's no way I'd even be heard. Second, I'd just be humiliating myself in front of people who almost certainly couldn't care less about anything I had to say. And finally, that even if I did somehow manage to form an intelligent argument that could be heard all the way across the room, the spectacle of it all would almost surely get me immediately escorted from the premises. Which would almost certainly get back to hospital administration and end with me being fired or, at the very least, disciplined.

No, if I want to give Warren Rutherford a piece of my mind, it needs to be up close and personal. I down my fifth glass of alcohol, in the form of an expensive cabernet sauvignon. A potent one, as the longer he goes on, the more I drink, and the more convinced I am that I have to speak to him.

So when he descends the stage to a round of polite applause, I watch him return to his table on the right of the stage as waiters start to make the rounds with desserts and coffee. So I know exactly where I need to go.

I stand up, make some excuse about needing to stretch my legs, and start walking along the back wall to approach his table from the side. No need to make more of a scene than necessary.

I stumble more than once, and someplace in my drunken mind I realize I'm in no shape to have this conversation. But it's like something has taken over my body and I'm being propelled toward him. Though even the same part that knows approaching him in this fashion is a mistake wants to see this done on some level. And I know I'm not going to chicken out now. I'm going to tell Warren Rutherford exactly what I think of his little speech.

# CHAPTER 4

I've nearly made it. Thirty feet more and I'll be face to face with the head honcho. The president and CEO of the Rutherford Group. The man whose name is on the hospital I've worked at for sixteen years. The hospital that's now so poorly run it's a joke. One I'm about to let him in on, since he seems to be under the impression that it's a paragon of advanced medicine and a jewel in the crown of his empire.

As I pass the table just before his, I'm grabbed hard around the wrist as someone rises from a seat next to me and stops me short of my goal.

"Where do you think you're going looking like hell's fury?" a familiar voice murmurs in my ear.

I spin around, attempting to take my arm back, but am pulled gently but firmly toward the speaker. Noah comes into focus as I look up into his face and read a warning there.

"Let me go," I insist as quietly as I can.

Noah pulls his head back, wrinkling his nose. "You've been drinking. Quite a lot, by the smell of it. I'm not letting you go anywhere until you tell me where exactly it is you're planning on going and to what end." His tone is firm and brooks no argument, not that I exactly want to have one here. We're already getting a few looks from the people at his table. I wouldn't so much mind, but better to save that for the real show.

I jut out my chin defiantly. "Let's just say I need to correct a few bits of misinformation in Mr. Rutherford's speech," I reply, trying my best not to sound drunk and failing miserably.

And Noah *rolls his eyes*.

"Come with me," he demands, abruptly sliding his arm around my waist and leading me forward. It's practically impossible to resist. He's very strong and very right — I'm a little too inebriated to control myself.

So I'm not able to get away as he leads me through a door in the right wall, sharply around a corner, and into an office just behind the ballroom. Closing the door, he finally lets me go.

"What are you doing?" I demand nervously as he faces me with his back to the door.

"Keeping you from embarrassing yourself," he says bluntly, arching an eyebrow.

"I'm not that drunk," I protest, even though it's taking everything I've got not to slur my words. "And you don't even know what I was going to say."

His eyebrow climbs higher. "First, yes, you are," he replies. "Second, you forget that I work for the man. I know what he's like, Julianna, and it doesn't matter what you were going to say. You're an employee at one of his hospitals, and he doesn't like being challenged by his subordinates. Especially not in public. And your current state just makes that all the worse. Your cause was lost before you even started. So, you're welcome."

"Well, I must not be totally smashed, because that actually made sense," I grumble, sinking defeatedly onto a hard settee next to the door.

He sits down calmly next to me. "Does it even matter what he said? All that matters is they just raised millions of dollars for a good cause. Was it really worth ruining your career to correct him?"

I look up at his beautiful face, suddenly completely self-conscious of what a mess I must be.

"Someone needs to," I whisper as my eyes fill with tears. "Because it's not about the speech. Well, not just about the speech. If he really thinks Rutherford Hospital is state-of-the-art …" I shake my head. "I've thought about going to see him before tonight. He should know what it's really like. Not just for the employees, but for the patients."

Noah tips his head to the side. "Their numbers always look good, or so I've been told," he says slowly. "Why don't you tell me?"

"What good will it do?" I ask, running my hands distractedly over the soft fabric of my skirt.

"Maybe it'll make you feel better to get it off your chest," he suggests, leaning back and slinging an arm behind me.

I give him a wary look, not convinced. But what the hell — what do I have to lose? I'm certainly not going to lose my job for telling Noah. So I take a deep breath. And I let it all out. About how we've been understaffed for years. That our equipment hasn't been updated to the point that even broken machines haven't been replaced, much less functioning ones swapped out for ones that are faster, more accurate, and simply vastly superior technologically. All in the name of the almighty budget.

Which was great until they hired Cal. I leave out that I know exactly how big his signing bonus was. But I don't leave out that they hired him right before denying the other medical staff raises for the second year in a row. Or that

Sasha, a loyal employee of nearly a decade, was denied a promotion to a position we need filled to keep up with demand, to avoid employee burnout, and to relieve the doctors of unnecessary work. All for, in the grand scheme of things, a mere pittance over what she currently makes.

By the time I'm done, I do feel better. And, at the same time, so much worse. Because if nobody outside of our hospital — well, besides Noah — hears about it and does something, it'll impact so much more than just my job. Because it's undeniable at this point. The hospital won't survive if something doesn't change.

"Well, if that's all true, I understand why you felt the need to correct him," Noah finally says drily after I've finished.

"Of course it's true. Why would I lie?" I reply tiredly.

He lays a hand over mine, stroking the back gently with his thumb.

"You sound more clearheaded now," he says gently. "Do you feel better?"

I take a deep breath and straighten up, letting my hair fall back over my shoulders. "I do. Thank you for listening." I give him a stern look. "Are you going to let me leave now?"

A slow smile spreads across his face. "If I let you leave, do you promise to stay away from Warren Rutherford?"

"The urge has passed," I assure him. "Though I think it's just about the time I was supposed to meet someone on the terrace."

"Ah. Yes," he agrees, checking his watch. "A bit after, actually. So our distinguished leader has probably left the building anyway." I don't miss the sarcasm in his voice. He rises, offering me a hand.

34

I stand, slipping my hand in his, trying to shrug off lingering anger. And feeling a little too sober for comfort.

"You look like you could use a distraction," Noah murmurs, looking into my eyes.

I look away for a moment, a swell of emotion churning through me. "Very much," I reply.

I feel his hand on my cheek, and I look back up into his eyes. From the desire on his face, I already know what his next words will be.

"I have a room upstairs."

And there it is. My insides clench at the implied invitation. And even though I'd already decided earlier that I would accept, I find myself unable to voice my response. So I simply nod.

His eyes harden and his hand closes around mine firmly. He leads me out of the room and to the elevators by the stairs in the main foyer. We ride quietly, hand in hand, up nearly twenty floors before it stops. His silent, steady presence is calming, and I follow him gladly down a long hall until he pulls a keycard out and opens one of the doors at the end.

We enter into a roomy suite, with a small, elegant seating area that connects to the sleeping quarters. The giant, fluffy bed at the back of the room looks like it popped right out of a fancy brochure.

I feel almost glamorous as he lets my hand go and turns to survey me. I may be exhausted, but I know what he sees as he takes me in. A woman in an expensive dress. Made up to look like the kind of woman I'm sure he's used to bedding. And I see a gorgeous man in an expensive suit who looks like he's going to devour me bodily before the night is over.

Normally he's everything I'd hate in a man. Clearly well-off. And though he's obviously intelligent, he's also bossy and more than a little arrogant. Not undeservedly so. But right now, I don't care. I'm happy to let him take charge. Because I need to let go. I need to not think.

I watch as he undoes his bow tie, letting it hang as he unbuttons his shirt, revealing hard pecs and a set of abs worthy of his gorgeous face.

I lick my lips in anticipation as he stalks toward me, slipping a hand into my hair and grabbing me by the back of the neck.

"You're beautiful, Julianna," he murmurs, his hand sliding behind me to find my zipper. He stares into my eyes as he gives a sharp tug. I feel the dress fall away, the cool air in the room sending goosebumps across my exposed back, stomach, and legs. It's an interesting contrast to the heat building between my legs as his hand trails down my back, coming to rest on the top of my thong.

I step into him, resting a hand on his chest, offering my mouth to him. I can't remember ever wanting to be kissed so badly. Ever being set on fire by so little contact.

He grips the hair at the base of my neck, tilting my head back. A small gasp escapes me as his mouth descends upon my neck, and I feel his tongue swirling up, to my jaw, his lips feathering across my cheek before meeting mine.

His hot mouth is hard and demanding, and I yield without thought. Our bodies meet, the solid plane of his chest pressed against my breasts as his tongue slips into my mouth. All the sensations are almost too much, and I'm dizzy with desire already.

Noah's mouth becomes more insistent upon mine, and suddenly his hands slip under my backside, lifting me to him. I wrap my legs around his waist as he turns and carries me to the bed, expertly mounting it on his knees and moving up to lay me on the pillows.

He undoes my bra, pulling away from my mouth so he can remove it. After it's been tossed to the floor, he pulls his own shirt and jacket off, throwing them after it. I rear up on my elbows, grab his belt, and quickly undo it, popping the button of his pants open before sliding the zipper down.

But I'm too impatient to wait any longer. I reach into his underwear, grasping, stroking, desperate to ready him. He watches patiently, the only sign of his enjoyment the tensing of his abs as I run a thumb over the moist tip of his cock. I pull it out, and the mere sight of it has me twitching in anticipation. But he's still not quite ready for that. Since he's too far over me for me to sit up, I use my other hand to pull his hips closer to my mouth.

"God, yes," he breathes, understanding what I want. He leans a hand against the giant headboard behind me and tilts forward so he's angled down, his expanding cock just over my face. With a grin, I open to him, giving a few sharp licks and sucks until I surrender.

He takes the cue, thrusting into my throat, his head tipping back with the pleasure of fucking my mouth. I encase him with my lips, enjoying the feel of him sliding over my tongue, getting harder on each thrust, until he's filled me to the point of gagging. I give him a few more seconds before pressing on his hip.

Obligingly, he backs off, swinging his body over me and standing next to the bed to pull off his trousers and underwear. The sight of his hard cock curling toward his abs has me soaking wet for him. I reach out and grab him, stroking as I stare him down.

"I need this," I beg.

He inhales sharply, grabbing my hand. "Careful what you ask for," he warns.

I prop myself up again, pleading with my eyes.

I can see him considering something, but after a few seconds he fishes a condom out of a bag I hadn't noticed in the open closet behind him. When he turns back to me, it's rolled down his length, and I lie back, practically vibrating with need.

He climbs over me. "I wanted the first round to go a little slower," he admits, prying my legs open and settling between them. "But you're just too damn sexy." He runs a hand between my thighs and groans.

"Obviously, I think you're pretty damn sexy too," I tease back, fully aware of how slippery wet I am for him.

"You haven't seen anything yet," he murmurs, pulling me toward him and lifting one of my legs as he fists himself. "But right now, I think we both need me to fuck you senseless, Julianna."

I arch off the bed at his husky, dirty promise. And before my back meets the mattress again, he's plunged into me so forcefully that my entire body clenches around him and a long moan escapes me.

He doesn't stop, though, and immediately starts fucking me so hard that I forget everything but him. And his cock. And his hands, which are caressing me everywhere he can reach as he takes me. It's sensory overload, and I fucking love it. My orgasm builds so quickly that I don't even have time to warn him before I'm screaming and clenching around him. But not even that stops him.

He continues to fuck another orgasm out of me a few minutes later with a well-timed caress of my clit. I throw my arms over my face, unable to look at how sexy he is without feeling like I'm going to come apart at the seams.

Never has a man taken me with such confidence. Never has my body responded to someone so voraciously. Never have I wanted to be owned the way he's owning me right now. But it feels out-of-this-world amazing.

Not even knowing it was possible, I'm aghast as he speeds up even more. I move my arms back down so I can watch him, the sweat sheening off his toned chest as his breathing accelerates. My legs start to twitch as a third orgasm builds under his intensity. I work my clit on my own this time, riding the wave of his efforts as I find my high. As I explode in body-melting bliss, I know he finds his release when he throws back his head and thrusts so forcefully into me I swear I'll be feeling it for the next week. In the best damn way possible.

He slumps forward while he catches his breath, then holds the condom in place as he pulls out. Once he's discarded it, he sinks onto the bed next to me, panting.

"I can't move," I say.

I feel his chuckle rumble through our touching arms.

"Good," he sighs. "Me neither."

After a few minutes of silent thought, I realize something out loud before I can stop myself. "I just had more orgasms in the last twenty minutes than I've had in the last two years."

He rolls onto his side, propping his head up on his hand.

"How's that even possible?" he asks curiously, with surprisingly little judgment.

"I'm sorry, were the cobwebs down there not a good warning?" I joke, rolling toward him.

He wrinkles his nose and shakes his head. "I think I know what the problem is. You have no idea how stunning you are, do you?"

I narrow my eyes at him. I'm not going to give this guy a hard time about being superficial. Not now. There's no point.

"My looks are beside the point," I explain. "I've just had too much on my plate for … any of that."

"There's never too much on your plate for orgasms," he replies seriously.

I slide toward him, running a finger down his chest. "Well, tonight I have nothing on my plate *but* orgasms," I say softly, looking up at him from under my eyelashes, trying to steer this away from my lack of a sex life these past couple of years.

Unsurprisingly, he takes the bait, smiling widely as he leans in and places a firm kiss on my lips.

"Perfect. What do you say we see how many we can manage?" With a wicked grin, he presses me onto my back, sliding down my body, trailing kisses all the way down to the still slick and now very sensitive warmth between my legs.

His tongue flattens against my sex, lapping at me until I'm aching and moaning once more. He goes at it like he means it, and it's not long before I'm coming from just his tongue. And he doesn't stop, slipping a finger into my pussy as I ride down the wave. I didn't expect it, and I buck my hips, a stream of curses flying from my lips. Still, he persists, stroking me until I settle into the sensation, then bringing me to orgasm again slowly with just his hand as he watches me.

"Five," he murmurs, kissing back up my belly, breasts, and neck. He slides out of bed and I catch sight of his cock, which is now hard again, and I pulsate with anticipation, knowing what he's out of bed to do.

Sure enough, he slips on another condom, and comes back to me. He helps me up, then turns me around, kneeling behind me and sliding in even though I'm tight and tender. But once he starts moving, it's only pleasure.

He pauses to gather my long hair in his hand.

"Your hair is fucking amazing, Julianna," he growls as he wraps it around his fist and uses it to pull me back onto his cock.

"Your dick is amazing, Noah," I growl back at him uncharacteristically. "Don't stop."

With a slam, he shows me that he clearly had no plans to. He pulls at my hair again until I have to lean back, and his cock presses down into my G-spot. I cry out and he wraps his other hand around my breast, working my nipple as he keeps me pulled taut with his hand and my hair and fucks me like an animal, hard and fast, from behind. Just when I think I can't take anymore, he switches it up, his hips pressed tightly against my backside, tilting so he rubs me inside until I'm building to a peak that has my whole body shaking.

"Let it out, baby," he urges through gritted teeth.

As if it was what I was waiting for, his command sends my orgasm tearing through me, triggering his as well.

This time when we sink down to the bed, sleep follows. Because you can't have six orgasms and not expect to need a nap.

# CHAPTER 5

Orgasms seven and eight happened after we'd had a few hours of sleep in the form of Noah going down on me again before another session of mind-blowing sex. Then number nine when we woke again around six o'clock this morning with slower, off-the-charts sensual sex. Now, at nearly seven o'clock, I'm finishing a quick rinse in the shower while Noah accepts room service breakfast.

I come back into the room naked because, well, all I have to wear is a lacy underwear set and a fancy dress. And oddly, I don't feel self-conscious being naked around him at all. Normally, I'm hyper-aware of my flaws with a man, but with Noah, even naked I feel gorgeous. Must be the effect of all the orgasms.

Breakfast has been set at the coffee table in the seating area, so I join Noah, who is sitting on the couch in his briefs munching on a piece of toast. His eyebrows jump when he sees me.

"Are you really going to eat breakfast naked?" he asks, though I can tell he hopes the answer is yes.

"Are you really wearing tighty-whities?" I tease, settling in the chair across the coffee table from him.

"Are you really complaining about seeing me in underwear?" he parries back with a cocky grin.

I roll my eyes. Of course he knows how good he looks in them.

"I can go put on a robe if it makes you uncomfortable," I reply airily.

"Don't you dare," he says in a commanding tone. Normally, that kind of bossiness would be a total turnoff, but coming from him it's … sexy. Damn him. "Eat. I need to be at work by nine, and I'd like to make it a round ten orgasms before that."

"You must be a supervisor or a director or something," I state.

He leans back, polishing off his toast. "Why do you say that?"

I raise an eyebrow as I pick up a banana and peel it. "Because you're clearly used to telling people what to do."

"I think informing someone that they're going to have another orgasm is a little different than telling people in an office what you expect of them," he says slowly.

I note he didn't deny that he's in some sort of position of authority. But he has that air about him, so he doesn't really need to confirm what's already obvious. Either way, I'm happy to let him think he has control. It's not going to matter in a couple of hours anyway. Still, I eat the whole banana, licking it suggestively as I do.

Noah shakes his head and laughs but waits for me to finish without saying anything.

"Enjoy the show?" I tease him.

"You're a little rebel, aren't you?" he murmurs back huskily. "Thinking you're so clever with that talented tongue of yours."

I shrug blithely in answer. Internally, I'm shocked by myself. How have I become this seductress? It's equally terrifying and exciting.

43

He rubs his thumb over his bottom lip, and I swear the expression on his face alone has me wet again. Even though I'm so sore, I still want him. I forgot what it was like, to want someone like this. Not that I think I've ever wanted someone quite so much.

Noah lifts his backside off the couch and slides his underwear off. His semi-hard cock bounces free, but he stops it with a hand, stroking himself up and down. I make to rise from the chair but he gives me a stern look.

"Sit down," he says, somehow making it sound both like a polite request and a command.

Either way, something in his tone makes me do it without thought.

"Good girl," he purrs. "Now put your legs up on the arms of the chair."

I look at him in disbelief.

"Just trust me, Julianna," he insists.

Still skeptical, I do as he asks, spreading my legs open for him. He eye-fucks my pussy from across the small space, and I feel my nipples harden as I watch him continue to stroke himself while he looks at me.

"Now, since you've obviously been neglecting masturbation, I'm going to give you a little instruction," he explains. "I'm going to tell you where and how to touch yourself, and you're going to do it. Understand?"

I inhale sharply, both totally turned on and instantly anxious. But I nod anyway, more interested to see how this plays out than I'd have thought I'd be.

He proceeds to issue various commands that have me touching my chest, my breasts, my stomach, between my legs. He asks me how each touch feels while he continues to work himself, breathing harder as I breathe harder. Stroking faster as I stroke faster. Until he's helped me find a way to stroke my clit — in hard swipes from right to left — that, in combination with all the touches that built me up, sends tremors through my entire body.

I don't know if he's really helped me unlock self-stimulation that actually does it for me like none ever has, or if watching him while he watches me is what's doing it for me. Either way, within about fifteen minutes, my tenth orgasm crashes through me as Noah erupts across from me. The sight of his cum squirting onto his hard stomach sends me careening back to my peak before I crash down, shaking and riding the intense pleasure still thrumming in my veins.

He tips his head back, resting it on the back of the couch as his erection recedes.

When the shaking finally subsides, I climb slowly out of the chair and move around the room, gathering my clothes and getting dressed while he watches me silently. Eventually, Noah heads into the bathroom to clean up. I guess that means it's time to get back to reality.

I slip the dress on, up over my hips, and hold it to my front. I pad into the bathroom as Noah finishes wiping himself with a towel and turn my back to him.

"Zip me up?" I ask softly.

With a small smile, he does, then turns me to face him. He strokes a hand down my cheek.

"I'm going to give you my phone number. Call me if you want to," he says.

I raise an eyebrow. "You're not going to ask for mine?" I ask. Then it occurs to me. "Ah. I see. You already have a girlfriend." After the words are out of my mouth, I hope to god it's not a wife.

But he laughs. "No, the only relationship I'm in is with my job," he assures me. "But I have a feeling if I asked for your phone number you'd either say no or give me a fake one."

A guilty look crosses my face before I can stop it, and he smirks at me as if to say, *See? I was right.*

What I don't say is that even if he gives me his number, I still won't call him. This was fun, but let's face it: It's not like I have the time or inclination to get into anything with him anyway. But regardless, I let him scribble those ten little digits down on a piece of hotel stationery, slipping it into my clutch before I put my heels back on.

"Thanks for stopping me from doing something stupid last night," I say as we stand at the door. "And, you know, for the rest." I can't help the grin that settles on my lips. It was a night to remember, that's for sure. And it's probably going to have to tide me over for a while. Though hopefully not another two years. Hell, maybe I *will* call him someday if I need another night stuffed full of orgasms to keep me going.

He steps into me, cupping my cheek in his hand. He kisses me with his usual abruptness, crushing his lips to mine in such a seductive way that I almost regret leaving. But he's not for me, I remind myself. Maybe nobody is.

"I hope to hear from you soon, Julianna," he murmurs.

"Goodbye, Noah."

And with that, I slip out the door without looking back.

# CHAPTER 6

"I don't know whether to be impressed or worried," Sasha admits after I've confessed everything over a late lunch on Sunday.

I chuckle. "Let's just chalk it up to drunken insanity," I joke, pushing the mostly uneaten food around my plate. "Seriously, I must've been crazy. I don't do that. Ever. And definitely not with a guy like him."

Sasha tilts her head and looks at me in that analytical way of hers. "Well, it's hard to know what he's really like, but no, I don't think I've ever known you to have a one-night stand," she agrees.

"Well, my dear, it's not the first time," I admit, ignoring the bit about what Noah is or isn't like. It's moot. "But then, that was a very long time ago, when I was young and frivolous. This felt anything but frivolous. I think it just needed to happen, if nothing else to distract me from the whole Warren Rutherford almost-mess."

"Oh, crap, speaking of almost-messes, I forgot to tell you," Sasha says, setting her water glass down with wide eyes. "MacDougall announced at yesterday's staff meeting that someone from the Rutherford Group is going to be joining the hospital administration team tomorrow to oversee some 'organizational restructuring.'" She does air quotes around the last two words.

"Noooo," I groan, sinking my face into my hands. "Not more budget bullshit!"

Sasha reaches over and strokes my arm reassuringly.

"So you'd heard about this? Are they really coming in to get rid of people?" she asks.

I drop my hands. "No, I hadn't heard, but I'm not surprised. Mrs. Knowles was promoted to director of the hospital, and she was the loudest proponent of budget cuts at last quarter's meeting," I grumble. I spread my hands out in defeat. "Guess that means she's getting her way."

"But why bring someone in from the Rutherford Group?" Sasha asks thoughtfully. "They haven't needed to do that before when letting people go. And lord knows there's been plenty of firings this past year."

"When staff-to-patient ratios dip below a certain level, they need approval," I explain. "Though I've never heard of them actually coming to the hospital to work with administration." I light up with a sudden thought. "Oooh, maybe they're going to fire one of the subdirectors or department chiefs. God, I hope it's MacDougall."

"I can't remember them ever having to do that, though," Sasha replies with a frown.

"Me neither," I agree. "But then, things have changed a lot. And not for the better. Because cardiac is already running understaffed. We simply can't afford to lose more people and keep up with our load."

"Preaching to the choir, sister," Sasha replies drily. "Now. Can I ask if you're going to tell Becca about your little fling? Since you clearly didn't invite her for brunch."

"I think you know I'm not," I admit, feeling a little guilty. I polish off my orange juice to hide my blush. While I may not be as private a person as Sasha is, which is why I know she'll understand, this is just something I don't want broadcasted. But I know it'll hurt Becca's feelings if she finds out and I didn't tell her. "At least, not right now. I love her, but she can't keep her mouth shut to save her life. And I don't really want it getting back to MacDougall that I turned his punishment into a sex-fest."

"If it helps, I think he's going to be a little distracted kissing Warren Rutherford's son's ass this week," Sasha says with a smirk.

My eyebrows jump. "Is *that* who's joining the admin staff? James Rutherford?" I ask.

"If that's Warren Rutherford's son, then yes, that's the rumor," she says.

Our waiter appears, dropping off the check and asking if everything was okay as he clears our plates. With our assurances that it was great, even though my food was barely half-eaten, he smiles and leaves us to return to our conversation.

"Well, he's director of finance for the Rutherford Group, so that makes sense in a way, I guess," I say thoughtfully. "But wow. That kind of seems like using a bazooka as a flyswatter."

"I didn't even realize his son worked with him until I heard that on Friday. Do you know anything about him?" she asks.

I fill out the tip and sign the receipt as I try to recall the little I've heard about him. Setting the black holder aside, I lean my elbows on the table.

"Just that he's a massive playboy," I say. "He's in the local society pages a lot for all the events he goes to. The women he dates. But I haven't heard much about him professionally."

"Is he hot?" Sasha asks bluntly, and I have to laugh.

"You're the last person I'd thought would care about that," I tease her.

Sasha rolls her eyes. "*I* don't care, but I know Becca is going to. Just trying to mentally prepare for nonstop comments if he is," she explains.

"Yeah, I thought that would die down now that she's with Vincent, but she still seems to be as vocal about good-looking guys as ever," I muse. *But then, who doesn't love a little eye candy, I suppose*, I think to myself. "Yes, he's pretty hot. Same features as his father, but you know, younger. I think he's in his early forties. Black hair. Blue eyes. Rich as sin. So of course women love him, though probably not as much as he loves himself. Lord help me, I hope I can keep my mouth shut while he's around."

"Message received, you despise entitled rich boys," she replies with a laugh. "I'm sorry, Jules. I hope this doesn't make things even harder on you at work. But I'm here, okay? You can vent to me whenever you need to."

"Be careful," I warn hear teasingly. "I might make you live to regret that offer."

She laughs and we wrap up our lunch, each heading our separate ways. I spend the rest of the day with my parents at the nursing home, thanking god it's the one Sunday a month Katie takes off. Because I know she'd suss out my little affair in an instant.

Even without the pressure of her presence, my head isn't in what I'm doing. I'm mentally checked out as I flip between wondering what shitstorm I'll be walking into at work tomorrow and flashes of my time with Noah. By the end of the day, I'm so over having all this time to think and just ready to deal with whatever comes next. Best to start getting it over with.

# YOU CAN'T BUY LOVE

* * *

At our staff meeting first thing on Monday, we're told that there will be two mandatory attendance meetings this morning, one each for half of the hospital staff, to introduce everyone to our new addition, let us know more about the plan going forward, and to answer questions.

So, with little more than an hour's notice, MacDougall leaves it to me to divide our rota between the two meetings. He doesn't even ask about the gala, so clearly he's already distracted by this new development.

With Becca's help, we're able to rebalance our morning appointments to split the team evenly enough to manage. Since we don't accept walk-ins and there's nearly always a cancellation or two, I'm confident we'll be okay. It's been longer than I can remember — a decade or more — since our last all-staff mandatory meeting. Here's hoping they grant leniency if any of the emergency or maternity docs need to bow out, because it's not like we can turn those patients away or tell them to wait. But with the way things have been around here lately, I do wonder if there would be consequences. That's how bad things have gotten, and how out of line with reality administration's expectations are.

Still, just before eight o'clock, I head to the meeting, leaving Sasha in charge of the nurses' station. I purposely go by myself, as I know I'm going to have a hard enough time containing myself. No need for my bad attitude to rub off on anyone else.

I make my way to the sublevel, using the stairs, even though they come out on the cafeteria side. It means there's nobody else using them, and I have another minute or two to brace myself.

As I walk the long hall past the cafeteria to the auditorium, people are streaming out of the elevator and the south stairs toward the meeting room.

I see a few familiar faces but keep my greetings to a terse smile and a nod. I'm in no mood for banter. Thankfully, once I'm inside, the huge theater-style room is already almost full, so I'm able to take a seat near the back without being noticed. Not that in a room of more than two hundred people anyone's going to pay attention to me.

I can see Mrs. Knowles and her assistant, Lisa, preparing things on the small stage. I crane my neck, looking for the chiefs. I catch MacDougall's balding head in the front row, seated next to the maternity chief. There are a few others in their row, but I don't recognize any of them well enough to identify them from behind, fifty feet away.

With a shake of my head, I cross my arms and lean back in my seat, ready to hear exactly what James Rutherford is going to say before I decide whether or not I'll go totally off the deep end.

At eight on the nose, Lisa calls us to order and the chatter dies down.

"Thank you all for coming," Mrs. Knowles says from center stage, clearing her throat. It echoes through the microphone pinned to her shirt. "I'm going to get straight to it as I know you all have very important things to be doing." She pauses like she's expecting applause or something. What, does she want a fucking cookie for recognizing we have more important things to do right now? I barely contain my eye roll. Thankfully, she continues even without a reaction. "As your department chiefs informed you this past Friday, we will have the privilege of hosting a distinguished member of the

Rutherford Group, who will be here to assist us in a hospital-wide organizational restructure. Our role as Rutherford's staff will be to fully support this effort to make our hospital run more efficiently and more smoothly." I nearly scoff out loud. *And by "efficiently," you mean "with fewer people,"* I think. "So, without further ado, I'll hand this over to our newest team member to introduce himself."

She looks pointedly at someone in the front row, who rises and climbs the stage. I'm too busy trying not to laugh at her use of the phrase "team member" to notice the person doesn't look like the pictures I've seen of James Rutherford until they turn around.

My heart drops into my shoes as he takes the microphone and pins it to the black suit jacket that's perfectly tailored over his broad shoulders, his full lips pulled down in concentration, his perfectly styled brown hair and gorgeous face unmistakable.

*Noah.*

But … no. What in the ever-loving-fuck is he doing here? I'm too stunned to do much but try to pick my jaw up off the floor as he looks up and smiles widely at the crowd.

"You're probably wondering why Mrs. Knowles didn't fully introduce me," he begins. "I wanted the chance to tell you a bit about myself. I've been the director of operations at the Rutherford Group for almost eight years now, working with our hospitals for another five before that. I specialize in organizational structuring, and since Rutherford Hospital is of particular importance to our group, I wanted to oversee this project myself. Now, there's no need to worry. I'm here to help. I want to make this hospital the absolute best it can be. And it's something I have years of success with, so please know you're in good hands." He winks at the crowd, and more than a few female titters ring through the room. His charm and commanding presence are palpable even from here, but rather than reassuring me, all I can feel is ice running through my veins. He spreads his hands invitingly. "Now, I wanted you to know *me* before I told you my name. So you know I've got what it takes to help, and that I'm here for the right reasons."

The pieces click together in my mind. And there's only one reason he'd be going about it this way.

"You're Noah *Rutherford*," I blurt out loudly.

Eyes the color of golden honey meet mine, and his smile falters for a fraction of a second as I see the recognition in his expression. But he's obviously well practiced at this, because his mask is back on in an instant.

"Yes, that's right," he agrees, as his eyes hold mine for a moment longer before they turn back to the rest of the crowd. And I feel like I've been punched in the gut. "But you can all call me Noah. I'm not here because I'm a Rutherford. I'm here because what you do is important, and I want to make sure we do everything in our power to support you. With that said, I look forward to meeting each and every one of you and addressing any concerns over the coming weeks. So I'll allow your chiefs to fill you in on the plan as it evolves, but for now I'm happy to answer any questions you might have."

I can't take it for another moment. Before I know what I'm doing, I'm on my feet and leaving the room. I don't even look back to see if he notices or cares. I can feel my anger rising, and I don't want to tempt fate.

I burst into the hallway, stomping all the way to the stairs, then fly up them in a rage. As I round the corner to a surprised Sasha, I simply shake my head in an attempt to discourage any questions. Unfortunately, Becca is also at the desk, and doesn't seem to notice, or doesn't care, about my obvious mood.

"That was over fast," she says, turning in her chair as I pace the floor behind her. "Well?"

"Well, what?" I snap.

Sasha raises her brows.

"Damn, girl," Becca says. "What's got your panties in a twist?"

I stop pacing and cross my arms over my chest. "Our new administrator isn't *James* Rutherford," I say pointedly to Sasha. "It's *Noah* Rutherford." I give her a meaningful look.

She looks askance at Becca, then back at me. "*The* Noah?" she asks quietly, her tone laced with concern.

I nod curtly, then scrub my hands over my face. I drop them to find Becca looking between Sasha and me.

"Okay, what's going on?" she asks sharply. "Why is he *The* Noah?"

Sasha looks to me desperately.

"I … met him at the gala. He stopped me from giving Warren Rutherford a piece of my mind after I'd had too much to drink. What he didn't tell me was that he was his son," I explain, giving her as much of the truth as I'm willing to right now. "I didn't even know Warren Rutherford had two sons." I press my lips together, trying to master myself.

"So?" Becca asks with a shrug.

I sigh and roll my eyes. "I vented to him. Told him everything I wanted to say to his father. I never would've done that if I knew who he was. Because clearly it made him want to take a closer look at the hospital."

"That's … not a good thing?" Becca hazards.

I throw my hands in the air. "Not if he's going to start firing people," I shout. A passing orderly shoots me a look. I lower my voice. "I'm sorry. I'm just pissed off."

Becca examines me for a minute, arms crossed over her chest. "There's something else going on here. I can count the number of times I've seen you visibly pissed off on one hand. Did this guy do something else to make you think …" She trails off and her eyes go wide as I see the moment the logical conclusion pops into her head. "Oh, Jules. Tell me it's true."

I freeze.

"It *is*," she hisses.

"Please, don't say a word. Especially not now, Becca," I reply harshly. "I can't take any more right now."

Becca mimes zipping her lips, locking them, and throwing away the key. Sasha taps her foots in thought.

"I am going to need details at some point though," Becca whispers. I shoot her a death glare. "I didn't mean now. Sorry." She mimes the zip and lock again, and it softens me just a little as I smile and huff a laugh through my anger.

"You know," Sasha interjects abruptly. "I'm kind of with Becca. Maybe it is a good thing. Maybe he really heard you."

I shake my head. "The guy's as arrogant as they come. And clearly not honest. He spouted all the usual corporate bullshit that spells layoffs. I've seen it enough times to know the deal, ladies. I'm sorry to say it, but it's just the truth."

"Well, shit," Becca says blandly. "This just got a whole lot less fun."

"You're telling me," I murmur, looking down into my hands and blinking tears out of my eyes. I can feel them watching me, and I'm back to pissed off in a heartbeat. I look up and shoot them death glares. "Well? Don't you two have things to be doing?" The sharpness of my tone sends them both scurrying about their business. And I do my best to focus on mine and forget Noah Rutherford even exists.

Noah *Rutherford*. How could I not ask his last name? How could I not realize? Stupid doesn't even begin to cover how I'm feeling. Like a complete and utter moron is closer to home. But also, totally terrified of whatever happens next.

# CHAPTER 7

I spend the rest of the day waiting for Noah to appear around every corner I turn, in every common area I pass through. By nearly three o'clock I'm seriously considering feigning illness so I can go home and hide. Unfortunately, that's not a long-term solution. Nor does it stop Lisa from finding me as I'm about to head in to see a patient.

"Hey, Jules," she greets me as she approaches the counter.

"Hey, Lisa," I reply, rising from my chair. "I'd ask how you've been, but I imagine you've got your hands full at the moment." I give her a sympathetic smile.

"You have no idea," she agrees with a heavy sigh that puffs out her chubby cheeks as she brushes her wavy brown hair out of her face.

"Well, I'd love to hear more about it, but I have an appointment to get to. Was there something you needed?" I ask pointedly.

"Oh, right, sorry," she replies, blushing. "Mr. Rutherford would like to see you in his office at the end of your shift. He's two doors down from Betty."

I raise an eyebrow. First, because I know for a fact Mrs. Knowles would be furious if she heard Lisa use her first name. Second, is he seriously summoning me to his office?

He really is an arrogant jerk if he feels the need to rub this in my face.

I briefly contemplate having her tell him to go stuff it but nix the thought just as quickly. Might as well clear the air now and let him know exactly what I think of his omitting his last name when he seduced me.

"I see," I reply tersely. "I'll see him around six then."

Lisa nods, but I don't wait for any further response. I turn and head to meet my patient, trying to shove my boiling rage deep down. I can't let this affect my job.

Except it already has. And I have a feeling it's not going to get a lot better from here.

\* \* \*

I stand at his office door for a full five minutes, staring at the muted-orange slab while taking deep breaths. I don't know if I'm more nervous or angry. Knocking seems like a bad idea. But so does leaving. Knocking it is. I rap hard three times, and my pulse kicks up about fifteen notches.

"Come in," he calls.

Great, he can't even be bothered to get up and answer his damn door. With a sigh, I turn the knob and enter. He doesn't look up. Sat behind a hospital-issue gray metal desk, his eyes are fixed on the laptop in front of him, the sleeves of his white button-front shirt rolled up to his elbows, displaying his toned forearms. Memories try to push their way to the surface of the last time I saw him using those forearms, but I shove them back and focus.

"You wanted to see me, *Mr. Rutherford?*" I say with more than a little sarcasm, standing in front of his desk and folding my arms over my chest.

That gets his attention. His light brown eyes dart up with a look of disapproval. He closes the lid of his laptop and gestures to the chair next to me.

"Have a seat," he instructs, rising from his chair. As I sit down, I watch him rise and round the desk, closing the door to his office. My stomach flips with nerves, and I can't tear my eyes from him as he returns to his seat. He leans back, resting one arm on the armrest and crossing his legs while he considers me. "You didn't call."

I let out a dry laugh. "No, I didn't. Is that a first for you?" I shoot back.

"You're pissed. I get it. You have every right to be." He looks so damn calm it riles me even further.

I tap my finger on the metal armrest of the chair, willing myself not to rise to any bait he dangles. I decide on the spot that there's no use asking why he didn't tell me his last name. Or what he planned to do with the things I told him. He's clearly untrustworthy, so whatever bullshit he comes up with just doesn't matter. What does matter is what he plans to do next.

"Is there something work-related you wanted to talk to me about? Because otherwise, I don't think there's anything for us to discuss," I respond.

"I hope you understand that I couldn't let what you told me pass, Julianna," he says firmly.

"Well, *Mr. Rutherford*," I say pointedly. "While I can understand why you felt the need to take action, I do hope you'll fully consider *everything* I said before making too many cuts."

I can practically see his defenses rise as he uncrosses his legs and sits up straight in his chair. "I'm here to fully assess the operating needs and personnel of this establishment, *Ms. Magnusson*," he snaps back, "and I'll do whatever I deem necessary to bring things in line with the Rutherford Group's plans for this hospital."

I snort. "That's not what you said in your pretty little speech this morning," I point out. "But then, I shouldn't be surprised. Bossy, arrogant, *and* you talk out of both sides of your mouth. I should've known you were a Rutherford from the start."

His nostrils flare and he leans forward. "I'm here because I'm good at what I do. And clearly this place needs to be taken in hand if employees would rather whine about their jobs than go through the proper channels to see things improved."

A shot of adrenaline courses through me, but I control myself. Though my voice shakes as I reply, "You have no idea who I am, how hard I've worked to do exactly that, and to look after my nurses and patients all at the same time. This place needs someone who cares about the staff. Who considers how much of ourselves we put into our jobs. It doesn't need someone coming in and making decisions about who stays and who goes neither knowing nor caring about what's been really happening, and who is really at fault for the current situation. Maybe if you pulled your head out of your privileged, know-it-all ass, you'd realize that the problem *started* with your almighty 'proper channels.'"

By the time I'm done, I'm shaking with anger, but I hold his gaze, unwilling to show weakness. And unable to believe that I spent an entire night with this man. Which just further proves that one-night stands are a very, very bad idea.

He leans forward onto his arms, fixing me with a dangerously stoic expression. "I called you in here hoping we could agree to move forward amicably. But let me make one thing clear," he says, carefully enunciating each word. "If you ever speak to me like that again, you'll be fired on the spot. If employees have been allowed to talk like that to their superiors, then I think I may have had exactly the right idea of what's been going on here. So if you can't show respect, learn to hold your tongue."

"I see, much like your father, you don't like to be challenged by your subordinates," I reply before I can stop myself. "I show respect where it's earned, Mr. Rutherford." I rise from my chair, knowing I need to leave before I push it too far, if I haven't already. I give him one last look, sadness overtaking me for just a moment, wondering where the man who made me feel like a goddess is. Or if it was all just an act. A lie.

I turn to leave.

He doesn't stop me.

# CHAPTER 8

I don't say a word to anyone. Not even Sasha, even though I know she'd be sympathetic. I just feel like talking about Noah and this whole mess would breathe more life and energy into it. So instead, I carry on as usual, ensuring the cardiac unit runs as smoothly as it can, putting that first. It means, at least, that there's too much to take care of to spend any time being angry at Noah Rutherford. Or time to wonder what curveball he's about to throw the hospital, or me, next.

The rumor mill is in full swing, wondering the exact same thing, so I know if so much as a pin drops out of place in the hospital, I'll hear before its echo has vanished. Though there's plenty of talk about the hot new addition to the administration staff. *That* I ignore as much as humanly possible.

The week continues eerily quietly. On Wednesday, MacDougall asks me to provide a full inventory, staff rota, our appointment schedule for the next three months, and our patient statistics for the last year. I barely bite back a snappy question about when exactly I'm supposed to do all that with everything else on my plate. I know exactly where the request is coming from, and I don't want to give our new overlord any reason to come looking for me or be dissatisfied with our unit in any way. If we're really lucky, maybe we'll come out of this relatively unscathed.

It's a lot to hope, I know.

I manage to get it all together by the end of the week, though MacDougall still grumbles about how long it took. And again, I somehow hold my tongue, not wanting to point out that *he's* our chief and he should really already have all that data or be able to easily assemble it on his own. But he's long "delegated" any real responsibility out. As far as I know, he spends his days seeing only his favorite patients and playing games on the ancient desktop computer in his office.

At nearing seventy with vision and hearing issues that would prevent him from performing surgeries — not that he was ever a particularly great surgeon anyway — it's only his grasp of politics and his in with the current administration that has kept him from being forced into retirement. But given how entrenched he is, I have no illusions about getting rid of him. They'll let me go long before they get rid of Malcolm MacDougall. Doctors of his experience and stature come with legend and tenure that outstrips even the most hardworking of the nursing staff.

On some level, I get it. A well-trained doctor is difficult to replace. But so is someone who actually gives a shit about the hospital.

I'm so irritated that I even skip the Friday evening team happy hour at our usual bar a couple of blocks away from the hospital. It's all happy couples now anyway, save me and a few others. One of those "others" being Ethan Malone, a nurse in our unit, who has always followed me around like a lost puppy. Well, me and several others on a rotating basis. But now with Sasha, Becca, and Harper all taken, I'm fearful of becoming his sole focus.

He's adorable in a little brother kind of way, though he's actually about my age. But with everyone pairing off, I feel his stares more now. And I can't even think about drinking alcohol anymore around a guy without being reminded of my last booze-soaked mistake of a night. Not that I'm in any way attracted to Ethan. Not like I am to Noah. *Was, Jules, was*, I firmly remind myself. Ugh.

I don't have time to consider what a bad place I'm in mentally before I head to the nursing home on Sunday morning. Katie is going to have a field day once she finds out what's happened in the last ten days.

But as soon as I walk in, she approaches me with a concerned look that freezes me in my tracks.

"What's wrong?" I ask, not bothering with pleasantries.

She lays a hand on my arm and stands close. "Your father's had some changes the last few days," she says quietly. "His trouble swallowing caused him to choke on Friday. He definitely got something down his windpipe and has been coughing since."

I internalize a sigh. "Any sign of fever?" I ask grimly.

She shakes her head. "Not yet. We'll get him scanned first thing on Monday in any case."

"Okay," I say softly. "Thanks for letting me know."

We stare at each other somberly. We both know this could lead to a lung infection. Which would almost certainly lead to pneumonia, given that he's eighty and has been battling this disease for so long. He's already having trouble getting proper nourishment with his swallowing issues. Complications like this are all too common at this stage, unfortunately. He's been lucky, really, to manage as well as he has for so long. It's been more than a decade, and his neurological decline has been steady, so we knew one of his symptoms would lead to more serious problems at some point.

Still, Katie gives me a lot of space, and I spend more time with Dad than usual, observing him and trying to keep him hydrated and comfortable.

As we're cleaning up from lunch, Katie smiles softly. "Why don't we talk about something else?" she offers. "How are things at the hospital?"

I level an impatient look at her. "That's not exactly an improvement in the conversation," I respond drily.

She chuckles tolerantly. "Well, I'd ask you about your love life instead, if you had one, but we both know that's …" She trails off as she takes in my expression and what I can feel is the extreme blush that's covered my face. A knowing smile creeps across her face. "Oh, ho ho. Well. I guess we *do* have other things to talk about, eh?"

"Is there any chance we could just not?" I grumble, turning to finish putting the dishes away.

"You pick. Hospital or love life. We can talk about whichever you want," she replies airily.

"Unfortunately, it's kind of the same conversation," I finally reply with a sigh, turning back toward her as I toss the drying towel on the counter. I throw it a little too forcefully, as it ricochets off, flying over the countertop and into the main area.

"Well, this ought to be good," she replies as she retrieves the towel. She places it gently on the counter and leans against the sink, staring at me expectantly.

I hold my breath, the pressure to spill my guts building until it's like a dam waiting to burst. Because I need to tell someone. To complain to someone.

"MacDougall made me go the annual charity gala last week, and I ended up sleeping with Warren Rutherford's son," I blurt out. "Except I didn't know it was him. He stopped me from drunkenly confronting his father, then I told him everything I hated about the hospital and how it's run before going back to his hotel room that night. Then Monday morning he shows up at the hospital, apparently to 'restructure,' and now I'm not sure if I'm more scared or angry. It's just a mess, Katie. I've made a bad situation worse, and I have no idea what to do now."

Her brow furrows. "James or Noah?" she asks.

"Huh?" I ask, totally taken aback by her response.

She shakes her head, picking up the tray full of medication she'd prepared earlier and gesturing for me to follow her.

"Which one of his sons?" she repeats. "James? Or Noah?"

I shake my head. "How did you even know he has two sons? And their names? *I* didn't even know that. And what difference does it make which one? I just gave my career a good, hard shove over a cliff."

Katie chuckles and ignores me as we enter the first room and she sees to her patient. On our way out, she gives me a smug smile.

"You forget," she says. "I worked there, all those years ago, when it was just Rutherford Hospital. No Rutherford Group, nothing to distract Warren Rutherford from pouring his heart and soul into his first hospital. Those boys lived in those halls once they were old enough to do real work, and I got to know them both quite well. And while certain things change as we age, our basic personalities stay quite the same from babe to …" We enter my mom's room and she gestures at my mother's grimace on our entrance. She's always hated taking medicine. "Well, old age. As you can see."

I gently help ease Mom's anxiety by rubbing her back and humming the "Spoonful of Sugar" song from *Mary Poppins* that she'd sing to me every time she made me take medicine as a child. And though I know she can't consciously remember since her dementia took most of her memories not long ago, it still soothes her. Proving Katie's point. On some level, we are always who we are deep down, our experiences and feelings somehow coded into us even when we can't recall them anymore.

I blink tears from my eyes as we leave the room.

"Noah," I reply softly.

"I thought it might be," she replies. "James was vain, even as a teenager. I imagine he's even worse now. Hard to see you going for someone like that."

"And Noah? He's arrogant, a bully, and a liar. Hard to think I went for someone like that. Even if it was only one night," I grumble.

She gives me a questioning look as we enter the next room. "That sounds nothing like the young man I remember," she says, handing a small paper medication cup to the waiting elderly patient. "He was honest to a fault. And very serious. A little too serious, if you ask me."

"Good thing I didn't," I reply snarkily, helping the resident with their water as Katie takes the empty cup back.

"Except you said you have no idea what to do now," she points out. "But if you're done with your little pity party, I'll tell you what I think you should do."

I put my hands on my hips. "Okay, Yoda, what do I do now?" I gripe.

"Noah Rutherford was always very self-contained and hardworking. He worked best alone, calling the shots. He could walk into a unit, take stock, then have the place in order top to tails within weeks. No fanfare, no talk — he'd work quietly behind the scenes with the people who could actually get things done while James schmoozed and talked up a storm with everyone else. He never said as much, but I could tell it got on his last nerve."

"So what does that have to do with me?" I ask.

"If you want to avoid career suicide, you need to figure out what Noah's trying to do and help him do it," she says plainly. "Because right now, he's seen you drunk and whiny, and you need to show him that's not what you're about. Otherwise, when he cleans house, you'll be on the list of things that go."

I squirm, uncomfortable with that level of honest and direct statement of fact. She's right. The night we met wasn't my finest hour.

"That didn't seem to bother him when he decided he wanted to see a lot of other things about me," I grouse.

"Sounds like neither of you were thinking entirely with your heads that night," she points out. "But if he's still the person I knew, he's not going to do things that are against the best interest of the hospital."

"Except he said he was going to do what was in the best interest of the *Rutherford Group*," I reply, "not the hospital. What if he makes things worse?"

"You say that like it's not in the Rutherford Group's best interest to improve things at the hospital," she insists. "I find it hard to believe that'd be the case. So think of it this way: What if he makes things better? Does it matter how he goes about doing that?"

"Yes," I insist, my brain spinning through all the horrible things he could do in the name of improvement.

"Why? Because you know what's best and he doesn't?" she asks, raising a brow. "You're more like him than you know. You have to be the one calling the shots all the time or you're not happy." She shakes her head and continues down the hall. But I'm left standing there, mouth open.

I accused him of needing to earn my respect. But she's right; that's a two-way street. I've done nothing to earn *his* respect. I've whined, I've jumped into bed with a man I hardly knew, then I blew my lid and acted like a bitch in his office. Granted, not without cause, but if I didn't know me, I wouldn't have much respect for me either.

Fuck it all, Katie is right.

I'm going to have to make nice with the arrogant asshole who may or may not be out to destroy everything I've worked for.

# CHAPTER 9

I return to work on Monday morning with renewed determination to take the high road and prove to Noah Rutherford that I'm not just a whiny employee. And hopefully to get in his good graces enough to be let in on whatever he has planned, so I can either prepare for it or jump ship before it's too late. I hope to hell it's not the latter.

At the morning meeting, MacDougall informs us all that Noah will be in our unit this afternoon to take a tour, meet everyone, and ask a few questions. I try to quash my nerves, but the tension must be obvious, since as soon as we're back at the nurses' station, Becca and Sasha both pounce.

"Okay, we've been leaving you alone on this, but I can feel your anxiety right now, girl," Becca says as quietly as she can, her eyes darting both ways down the hall.

Sasha nods in agreement, reaching out to gently squeeze my hand. "What can we do?" she asks softly.

I huff a dry laugh. "You girls are sweet, but I'll be fine. I'm sure I'll barely even have to see him, much less talk to him." They both give me skeptical looks. "*Really.* I appreciate the concern, though."

Suddenly, MacDougall materializes around the corner, causing us all to bolt upright and look like we were working all along.

"Ah, Ms. Magnusson. Good. I thought I should inform you that you'll be conducting Mr. Rutherford's tour this afternoon," he says, pompously staring down his old, crooked nose at me. "He'll be by at one o'clock."

Now my eyebrows shoot up, my chill totally gone. "I'm sorry, what?" I all but screech. I feel Sasha squeeze my hand hard, snapping me back to the reality of the situation. "I mean, of course, sir. Will you be joining us?"

"You can just bring him to my office when you're done with the formalities," he responds. "I'll take it from there."

And without waiting for a response, or even thanking me, he walks away. I have to take three deep breaths before I'm not seeing red.

"We'll take care of the schedule," Becca assures me.

"And I can ask Cal to do the tour with you," Sasha offers. "He's a great buffer."

I look between the both of them gratefully.

"Thank you," I say, breathing out a sigh. "But I'm sure Cal has more important things to do than hold my hand. Besides, I've been more or less doing a good part of MacDougall's job for years, might as well do this too."

"This is different," Becca says quietly. "We have to put up with a lot of bullshit around here, but you don't have to do this alone just to prove you can, Jules."

"Actually, I think I do," I reply.

Sasha squints at me. "For Noah Rutherford, or for yourself?" she asks insightfully.

I give her a dim smile. "Both."

* * *

# YOU CAN'T BUY LOVE

At a quarter to one, I'm trying to distract myself with paperwork when someone clears their throat. My eyes snap up to the counter. Noah. Of course he's early.

I take a deep breath, click save, lock my screen, and shut off my monitor.

"Mr. Rutherford," I greet him formally, rising and rounding the desk to meet him. "Welcome to the cardiac unit."

I try not to notice how handsome he looks in the plain tan slacks and navy button-front shirt he's wearing that, once again, has the sleeves rolled up to the elbow. And his shirt is again so well-tailored that it fits snugly against the muscles of his biceps and chest. Good lord.

"Nurse Magnusson," he replies with a polite nod. But his confused, darting glance betrays his cool tone. "Will Dr. MacDougall be joining us?"

I slip my hands into my pockets, willing myself not to laugh at his obvious discomfort. This might be more fun than I thought.

"I'll be conducting your tour before you meet with him," I reply. "Is there anything particular you'd like to start with, or shall I just show you around?"

"Is there a reason he asked a nurse to conduct the tour rather than doing it himself?" Noah asks testily.

"Nurse practitioner," I correct him. "And I'm afraid you'll have to ask him that yourself. If you'd like, I can take you to his office straight away instead?"

He considers me for a moment before giving a small shake of his head. "Lead the way," he says. His expression is unreadable, but I don't let it faze me.

With a well-practiced fake smile, I do just as he asked. I show him everything. The exam rooms, the observation rooms, the surgical areas. Storage, supplies, sterilization areas, equipment trolleys, the whole shebang. I walk him through our patient numbers, our typical staffing rotations, our interdepartmental transfers, everything. Well, almost everything — I skip the breakroom since that seems like a bit much.

We manage to snag a few minutes each with Dr. Carson, our senior cardiologist, and Cal, and Noah asks them each the same generic questions before continuing on our way.

He meets most of the nursing staff, all of the MAs, and a handful of orderlies who are shared with other departments.

After more than an hour of walking the entire unit while talking endlessly, with few questions from him, we finally circle back to the nurses' station. Becca sits at the desk, quiet as a mouse, but I know her ears are wide open.

"So that's everything I can think of," I tell him. "Did you have any further questions for me on our numbers or anything else we covered?"

Noah looks a little overwhelmed.

"Not at the moment," he admits. "Everything seems to line up with the reports I was given."

I snort. "It should, since I made those," I reply.

That gets an eyebrow raise. "When is the other ARNP scheduled again?" he asks.

"Nurse Marcus works night shift and Sunday," I respond. "She should be here around six. I think the only other staff member you didn't meet is Dr. Franklin, and he's on medical leave for knee surgery until next week. I think that covers everyone."

"Almost. What's Dr. MacDougall's patient load like?" he asks.

Becca coughs behind me and I purse my lips. "Well, he's our next, and last, stop," I reply. "I'm sure he'd be happy to discuss that with you."

Noah huffs a small laugh. "I'm asking you, Nurse Magnusson."

I rub my lips together, trying to figure out how to say this without putting myself in danger.

"Dr. MacDougall typically serves in a more administrative capacity," I reply hesitantly. "As such, he only sees established patients."

Noah nods slowly. And I'm pretty sure he understands exactly what's going on.

"Do you have any other questions for me?" I ask, itching to get this over with.

"No," he says. "But I will say, I've had a fair few conversations with the other chiefs and doctors in the hospital. Your name came up quite often."

I bite back a laugh. "Yes, well, I've worked here for sixteen years, in almost every part of the hospital," I reply with an affected shrug.

"Huh," he grunts. "Yes, well, that might explain things, as it usually came up when I asked who had the most knowledge of how things *really* work around here."

I try not to look smug. I really do. I'm not sure if I'm successful or not, because he just stares at me for a minute.

"Like I said, I've worked here a long time. And I do my best to listen to the people I work with to understand what's going on. I'm often involved in resolving interdepartmental issues."

"Seems like a lot of talk doesn't filter up the proper channels," he replies.

I hear Becca huff softly behind me, but Noah makes no sign that he heard her, so I try to pretend like it didn't happen and hope she doesn't do it again.

"Oh, it does," I assure him. "At the proper times. For example, we discussed many of those issues at our quarterly budget meetings last month."

That gets a startled look from him. "You went to *budget meetings*?" he asks incredulously.

"Well, I'm on the budget committee, so yes," I reply, folding my arms over my chest defensively.

"I wasn't aware nurses ..." He trails off at my steely glare. "My apologies. I wasn't aware that *nurse practitioners* were typically involved in budgeting."

Oooh, I got *his apologies*. I'm sure that doesn't happen often.

"Each department has a chief and one or two other representatives, based on department size, who are acquainted with the department's needs to properly represent that unit's interests," I say with a shrug. "Dr. Franklin hates dealing with financial matters and Dr. Thompson is too new to have a full understanding of everything. And Sarah — sorry, Nurse Marcus, prefers to keep her night hours, so she's not able to attend the meetings. So it's me and Dr. Carson. Is there an issue with that?"

"No, no issue at all," he murmurs, his eyes scanning my face. "I think I'm ready to speak with Dr. MacDougall now."

"Then right this way," I reply, gesturing to the corner left of the nurses' station. As he walks around it and out of sight, Becca holds up a hand as I pass. Suppressing a smirk, I reach out and high-five her as I walk by. Take *that*, Noah Rutherford.

\* \* \*

I'm with a patient later that afternoon when there's a knock on the door. I excuse myself and step out to find Sasha twisting her fingers anxiously in the hall.

"Mr. Rutherford wants to see you in his office," she says softly. "He called just now and didn't say when, so I thought it best to let you know immediately."

I shake my head. Here I thought he was starting to understand.

"If he calls back, I'm with a patient. I'll go up once I'm done, but you'll have to get Becca to have Dr. Carson or Cal cover my four p.m."

"I can take over now, if you'd like?" she offers.

I fold my arms over my chest and give her a stern look. "You're not doing ARNP duty unless you're *paid* to do ARNP duty," I respond. "But thank you."

With a weak smile and a nod, Sasha walks away, leaving me to return to my patient.

As I wrap it up, I can't help wondering if Dr. MacDougall said something to Noah that prompted this. I shake myself, trying to focus on the task at hand, instead of the sea of what-ifs.

It's not long before I'm heading up to Noah's office anyway, braced for whatever's coming.

His door is open when I arrive, but I still knock politely, hovering in the doorway.

"Come in," he calls without looking up. "And close the door behind you."

Oh. Fuck.

I swallow hard and do as he asks, sinking meekly into the chair across from him. He finishes whatever he was writing on the tablet in front of him, then throws the pen down, leaning back in his chair and crossing his legs.

77

"I owe you an apology," he says frankly, threading his fingers together in his lap.

I snort and say, "Several, by my count." Then immediately wish I could crawl in a hole and die.

But he doesn't get angry. In fact, he tips his head back and laughs. And damned if the sound, the absence of sternness from his expression, doesn't remind me of the Noah I met that first night. My insides tighten in a way that's totally contrary to the moment.

"Yes, probably," he admits, clearly amused.

I spread my hands. "What for?" I ask, trying to cover my gaucheness.

"For doubting you. I've reviewed your reports and, after speaking with nearly everyone in the hospital, everything you said to me at the gala was spot-on. Technology and staffing both have serious deficiencies."

Our eyes meet, and there's something more in his expression than an apology. It's the first time he's mentioned that night since our initial meeting here in his office. And something about the reference has injected a tension into the room that wasn't there a minute ago.

"I told you I wasn't as drunk as you thought I was," I murmur, not breaking eye contact.

He leans forward. "Yes, you were." His expression is intense. Intense like … a flash of his face while he was inside of me crosses my mind, and I inhale sharply. I've been so careful not to think about it since he showed up, but that one slipped through my defenses.

"Okay, maybe right at that moment I was. But not …" I stop, blushing, realizing that whatever I was about to say would be completely inappropriate. That everything I'm thinking is completely inappropriate. And suddenly, I remember Katie's advice. Taking a deep breath, I get my head back on straight. "But that's not the point. I'm glad to hear you understand the issues we're facing. What can I do to help?"

His lips pull into a small smile as his eyes roam over my face. Like he's remembering what I looked like while he fucked me too. I squirm uncomfortably in my chair, hoping I can regain some semblance of self-control.

"You can help me figure out how we get the employees to speak up more," he eventually replies.

And just like that, reality crashes in like a bucket of ice water.

"I'm sorry, did you not hear me earlier when I said they already are? Maybe you should be asking how we get leadership to listen. But that might be a touch too ironic."

Damn my mouth. I clamp it shut as I watch him assess me. Differently this time. Colder.

Not that I blame him. Why can't I control myself around him? I'm not one to pick fights, but I can't seem to help myself around him for some reason.

"Complaining to one another, and random strangers," he looks at me pointedly, "doesn't count. I'm talking about approaching their supervisors directly — privately — to report issues or concerns. Not broadcasting them to the grapevine and hoping that leadership will magically be able to separate fact from gossip. That can't be coming through one person, no matter how qualified she is. Each employee needs to be able to own their own voice or there's no knowing how much of a problem something really is."

"Uh, except by using your eyeballs, maybe?" I retort, totally ignoring his sort-of compliment. "You literally *just* said you've looked into things and came to the same conclusions I did. Why does it take loads of people complaining before the chiefs or directors act on something? Shouldn't *they* be the ones proactively looking for ways to make things run better around here?"

"They do have some responsibility, yes," he admits. "But they have many others that prevent them from being everywhere all at once. And I understand why they wouldn't rely on one squeaky wheel to be their only source of knowing when action needs to be taken."

I snort. "You mean I've worn out my welcome with MacDougall, so he doesn't believe me anymore."

"He does think you exaggerate, yes," Noah admits.

I throw my hands in the air. "Fine. Then maybe start directing leadership to stop punishing people who report issues. I'm the only one who does because I know they won't fire me. Or, at least, I care more about fixing things than being fired."

His brow furrows. "Punishing in what way?"

Oh, fuck. I know I've stuck my foot in my mouth now. Because no matter how I answer this, I'm screwed. If I backpedal, I prove MacDougall's point that I'm exaggerating. If I tell the truth, I'm speaking negatively about my bosses without any way to prove that I'm being honest. And clearly Noah Rutherford is all about proof.

How do I convince him that they've fired people for less? That they often fire people simply to replace them with friends, or children of friends, or people who are willing to kiss their asses? That nobody wants to give them any excuse to get rid of anyone who isn't indispensable? How can a man like Noah Rutherford understand any of that when he's likely only in the position he's in because of his name, even if he is good at what he does?

Instead of asking all these questions out loud, I sit silently, giving him a pleading look. Asking without words that he not make me voice these things.

I've never felt so powerless as his eyes demand answers. But I have none to give.

"You're not going to tell me, are you?" he finally murmurs.

I shake my head, looking down into my lap. A few tears fall onto my hands, and it makes me angry. Angry that I've shown vulnerability in front of this man. This man who I was so happy to be vulnerable with not so very long ago. But that was when I had no idea who he was or what he was capable of.

With a sigh, he rises, opening his office door. I stand at the clear dismissal, not meeting his gaze. Too upset to acknowledge his power in this moment.

"I can't help if you don't talk to me," he says as I pass him.

I freeze, but I don't turn around.

"Sometimes being a leader means helping people who are too afraid to use their voices," I say, my own voice strained.

"Julianna," he breathes softly.

And I turn and catch his eye before I can stop myself. My fragility in this moment is reflected in his eyes. I can see that he's struggling. That he doesn't know what to do. But I have a feeling it's about more than what we'd been discussing. And I don't know what to do about *that* either.

He steps toward me, raising his hand to brush a tear from my cheek. I don't flinch or make any move to stop him. It feels too good to remember what it's like when he touches me. Even if it's just a small touch. A single moment.

"I see how much you care about this place," he says, looking down into my eyes. "You can trust me, I swear. I'm not trying to make this harder on you."

"How can I trust you when you didn't believe me in the first place?" I point out.

"Because trust, like respect, is earned," he replies firmly. "And for what it's worth, you've earned both from me."

My lips part and my eyes close.

"But you haven't earned mine," I whisper.

I reopen my eyes and look up at him. I knew there would be hurt in his eyes, but I wasn't prepared for what that would make me feel. That I feel for him at all. This is all so … messy.

"I will," he promises.

I feel his hand slide around mine, then he lifts it to his lips. He places a kiss on the back of my hand, transporting me back to the moment we met. A moment filled with hope. But this time I don't swoon. Because I know exactly who he is now. And though hope still blooms somewhere inside me that this whole situation will work out for the best, I can't see it ever working out with him. No matter what my traitorous heart says.

# CHAPTER 10

"I still don't know why being a Rutherford counts against him," Sasha insists as she twirls her martini glass on the small bar table. Even though it's a Tuesday night, the place was still too packed to snag a booth. "Shouldn't that mean he cares *more* about the hospital?"

I shake my head. "I wish that were true," I reply. "But if it were, why would things be the way they are now?"

"I'm with Sash," Becca pipes up. "Dude may be a daddy's boy, but they can't afford the bad press if they start tearin' shit up."

"Except every employee has signed NDAs, so how would anyone ever know?" I point out. Granted, those are supposed to be for patient confidentiality, but it extends to all hospital business.

"Pfff," Becca scoffs. "Please. I could drive Vincent's truck through the loopholes in that thing."

"Vincent lets you drive his truck?" Sasha asks curiously.

Becca shrugs and I wave a hand. "You're both missing the point. Just because he's a Rutherford doesn't mean he's going to make things better. The Rutherford Group is all about the bottom line. Sure, it may have started to help people, but they've long since focused more on profitability and appearance."

"Well, they clearly don't pay attention to staff complaints," Sasha agrees drily. She raises her glass. "Here's hoping we're not all looking for jobs by the time this is all over."

"I'll drink to that," I say, lifting my highball glass to meet hers.

"Hell, I'll drink to anything," Becca jokes, her pint glass meeting ours.

We all take a drink, then Becca sets hers down and rubs her hands together.

"So, are you planning on jumping back into bed with Moneybags?" Becca asks with a lascivious grin.

"Nope, nope, nopety, nope, nope, nope," I chant. "I hadn't planned on it even *before* I found out who he was when he started working at our hospital."

"Awww, come on. Just because he's a jerk doesn't mean you can't hit that again," Becca whines. "That man is fucking *hot*."

"Becca, you think every man is fucking hot," Sasha points out.

Becca wrinkles her nose and sticks her tongue out at Sasha. "Do not. How many times did I turn Mark down?"

Sasha tilts her head. "Twenty-five? Thirty? I lost count."

"Precisely," Becca says matter-of-factly. "So don't go pretending like I don't have standards. Or that Noah Rutherford isn't delicious in those tight-as-hell shirts. Damn, that boy's got some muscles."

I choke on the sip of alcohol I'd just taken. Well. Guess I'm not the only one who appreciates Noah's workwear.

"Look," I hedge. "I'm not saying he's not attractive. Or that that night wasn't … well, it was phenomenal. Record-breaking." Becca raises an eyebrow, and I hold up a hand.

"But I've learned my lesson about dating at work. And even if I didn't, he's exactly not my type."

Becca looks insulted, and I know what's coming.

"First of all," she says, snapping a finger up, to count or for emphasis, I'm not sure which, "dating at work has turned out pretty damn well for us," she gestures between her and Sasha, "and second of all, girl, please. Rich and handsome isn't your type? But mostly … I'ma need to know exactly what records we're talking about here." She leans forward on her arms, eagerly awaiting my response.

I roll my eyes so hard it hurts a little.

"First of all, you don't *need* to know anything about that night," I mimic her, shutting that down real quick. "Second of all, *no*, entitled rich boys just don't do it for me." Such a lie. Well, in this case anyway. Because Noah very much did it for me. Ten times. "But mostly, I'm just past that phase where I'm open to risking my career for a man. No offense to either of you, but you both are fully aware of how badly that can blow up in your face."

"Well, you're not wrong," Sasha agrees hesitantly. "But we know you pretty well, Jules. And it feels less like you're not open to this because of who he is and more because, well, you've kind of just given up on the whole dating thing." She shrinks back into herself and shoots Becca a look, clearly begging for support now that the words are out of her mouth.

I open my mouth to protest, but Becca beats me to the punch.

"Don't even think about disagreeing with that," she says sharply. "You were severely dick-deficient for way too long. Try to deny it."

I purse my lips together, nostrils flaring. She knows I can't.

"That's right," she says smugly, crossing her arms over her chest. "So don't even pretend like you didn't enjoy it. Or that regular access to the D wouldn't vastly improve your life."

Sasha blushes bright red and hides behind her drink.

I shake my head, knowing it's impossible to argue with Becca.

"I'll take that under advisement. Can we talk about something else now?" I beg.

Becca happily launches into a story about Vincent and some cute thing he did last weekend, and I gratefully down the rest of my drink while she does, muttering encouraging noises and agreements here and there. Once she's exhausted, Sasha manages to catch us up on her life. And it feels nice to listen to them, to not think about my own crap. At least for one night.

* * *

The next afternoon I get a most unexpected voicemail on my cellphone telling me I've won the hot air balloon ride I bid on at the gala. Certain they must be mistaken, I call the number to correct them, only to be told that it was the annual "gimme" prize — the one auction item that *everyone* will win that year. Apparently it's a secret item that is different at every gala to try to get people to bid on multiple items in hopes of snagging the freebie. Who knew? I'm given an email address to contact the person who runs the rides.

And for the first time this week, I'm actually smiling as I compose and send an email. Though I'm also hoping I'll be able to manage to get it scheduled around work, a bit nervous that the sunset part of the "sunset hot air balloon experience" is toward the *end* of the ride. Which would mean the ride would start in the late afternoon. A near impossibility with my job. But nothing ventured, nothing gained.

To my utmost surprise, by the end of the day I've learned the person running it has an opening for Sunday. Saturday is the Fourth of July, and apparently the Sunday booking didn't realize they'd made it for the wrong day, thinking they'd get to see fireworks. Their stupidity is my gain, and I agree to meet at five o'clock, beyond excited. Also a first for the week.

* * *

On Thursday my high takes an abrupt cliff dive when, as I'm handing things off to Sarah that evening, MacDougall calls her into his office.

With a sick feeling in my stomach, I decide to hang around and wait to hear what he wanted. Sarah comes back not fifteen minutes later looking grim-faced.

I wait expectantly as her eyes follow one of the orderlies around the corner before she says anything.

"They're letting Caroline go," she tells me in a low voice.

"*No*," I gasp. "You're already short nurses on second shift. What the hell?"

She rolls her eyes as she pulls together a stack of files. "Apparently, we don't have enough patients to require more than one nurse."

I throw my hands up. "Like that's all you guys do. Who is going to handle sterilization, stocking, and setup?"

Sarah sighs deeply. "Zoe and I will get it done, don't worry," she assures me in an uncharacteristically snappish tone.

"Hey," I say, laying a hand on her arm. "I hope you know that's not how I meant it."

"I know," she agrees. "I'm just shaken up. The way he was talking … I don't know, Jules. I wouldn't be surprised if they get rid of me next."

My blood turns to ice. "Why would you think that?"

She glances both ways down the hall. "When I met Mr. Rutherford night before last, he asked if I thought we needed a full staff for second shift. If there needed to be *anyone* besides an on-call doc."

"But you told him about all the other functions you guys perform, though, right?"

"Of course I did," she scoffs. "He didn't seem convinced you guys couldn't handle that as part of first shift."

A boiling anger bubbles in my gut. "Then maybe he needs a little more convincing," I say heatedly.

"Don't do anything rash, Jules," Sarah says, a warning in her voice.

I give her a look. "Why, because if I get fired, then you have to work the day shift?"

She grins. "Can't get anything by you. Seriously though, I don't want you to put yourself in the crosshairs, okay?"

"You know me. I can't make any promises."

She gives me a concerned look. "Yeah, that's what I'm afraid of."

"Whelp, I'm done for the day. See you for morning handoff?"

"Mhm. See you tomorrow," she grumbles, heading to put away the stack of files she collected.

As soon as she's gone, I head for the elevator. Time to give Mr. Moneybags, as Becca so aptly named him, a little dose of reality.

# YOU CAN'T BUY LOVE

While I ride up in the elevator, I pull my ponytail loose. A sigh escapes me. It's a small dose of relief before I step into the lion's den. Hopefully he hasn't left for the day already. Though something tells me he'll still be here.

I find out quickly that I'm right, as I approach his open office door and see him on his cellphone, pacing the back wall of the small room. He runs a hand through his hair, clearly agitated as he talks business gibberish with the person on the other end.

I stop in his doorway, leaning against the frame as I watch him. It's more hypnotic than I'd like it to be, watching his muscles ripple under his shirt, his honey-colored eyes lit up and intense.

Then they land on me and my stomach does that damn flip-flop thing. Traitor. I wave meekly and he quickly ends his call.

"Julianna," he says, sounding half like a greeting, half like he's surprised to see me. He gestures at the chair across from his desk as he retakes his seat. "What brings you here?"

I approach, standing next to the chair, but not sitting.

"I think you know. How am I supposed to trust you, respect you, when you don't even bother to give me a heads up before firing one of my nurses?" I ask pointedly, my tone laced with as much disgust as I can manage.

"I wasn't aware I needed your approval," he responds sharply.

"You seriously didn't think I'd be a little unhappy with that?"

"Unfortunately I'm not here to make you happy, *Nurse Magnusson*," he replies.

My eyebrows shoot up. So that's how he wants to play it.

89

"We're really back here, huh?" I ask, shaking my head. "Fine. In case it wasn't obvious, second shift doesn't just sit around and twiddle their thumbs. We don't have the staff to manage their duties as part of first shift. I can give you whatever data you need to substantiate that. But I'd like you to reconsider letting Caroline go."

He's silent for a moment. Hopefully reconsidering. But when he rises from his chair and comes around the desk, leaning on its edge so he's right next to me and at my level, I have no idea what to do. His nearness is unsettling on several levels, and I can see darker amber flecks in his honeyed eyes. I swallow hard, suddenly unable to speak.

"What if I told you that letting her go is part of a bigger plan that I can't share yet?" he ventures.

"Short-term pain for long-term gain? That's what you want to sell me?" I ask, crossing my arms.

He grins, and it sends my tummy flipping again. Damn him.

"Yes, something like that," he admits.

"Except that would require me to trust you," I point out. "Which I don't yet."

He raises an eyebrow. "You said 'yet,'" he replies, sounding a bit shocked. "That's progress, Nurse Magnusson." This time when he says my name, it doesn't sound like an admonishment. It sounds ridiculously sexy. And I suddenly feel like the temperature in the room has jumped a good ten degrees.

"You're not going to flirt your way out of this," I insist. But even I note that I don't sound particularly convincing.

"No?" he muses, his eyes searching mine. He rises, towering over me. He's taller than I remember, but then, the last time we were this close, I was wearing heels. "I guess you'll just have to wait until I can prove it to you, then."

"What does that mean?" I ask warily.

"It means, if you can't trust me, at least give me some time," he replies.

"But you're still going to let Caroline go."

"Yes, I'm still going to let her go."

I narrow my eyes at him. I can't honestly say Caroline was our most productive nurse, and if I'd had to pick someone to go, it probably would've been her.

"Fine," I reply tersely. "But don't be too long about it."

I turn to leave, but he catches me by the elbow. I look back up into his eyes, which are now so filled with intensity it takes my breath away.

"Don't look at me like that," I whisper. But I can't move, pinned in place by his gaze.

"Then don't come in here with your hair down," he whispers back. He reaches up and runs his hand down the locks tumbling over my shoulder and along my arm. Shivers race up and down my spine.

"Noah …" But even I have no idea what I was going to say.

"Why didn't you call?" he murmurs.

"Why does it matter?"

"I don't know. It just does."

I pull back. "I'm sure you'll get over it. As it is, if it wasn't off the table before, it certainly is now."

"It doesn't have to be," he replies.

"Yes, it does."

"Why?" he insists.

"Why won't you let this go?" I retort. "I'm sure there are a million other women who would happily hop into bed with you." It comes out angrier than I intend, but I don't like him putting me in this position.

But Noah looks sincerely offended. "I'm not my brother, I don't sleep with just anyone," he says.

"Just employees who can't say no?"

"You can say no. You do say no. Quite often, actually," he points out.

"I'll keep saying it until you listen. But it's not fair for you to keep asking, given your position. You must realize that," I throw back at him.

"You're right," he admits, leaning back against the edge of the desk and giving me a little breathing space. "It's not fair. But then, you're not exactly being fair either. You were fine sleeping with me when you didn't know my last name."

"That wasn't usual for me either," I respond. "Believe me."

"I do. It was special. This," he gestures between us, "is something. You're not the least bit curious if it's more than good sex?"

"No," I lie. And I have to stop myself from correcting him that it was *great* sex.

He laughs. "Damn, you're stubborn."

"Yep. So you might as well give up now."

He pushes up off the desk, looking down at me. "Is that what you want? For me to give up?"

I throw my hands up. "I've only been saying it this whole time," I reply in exasperation. "But I guess you weren't listening."

"Oh, I heard you, loud and clear. But the thing about reading a person is not just listening to their words," he replies, his eyes fixed intently on mine. "It's also their body language. How fast they're breathing." He pauses pointedly, and the bastard is right. I'm practically panting. "The blush of their cheeks." Fuck him, he's right again, and it only makes me blush harder. "Sometimes our bodies betray us, Julianna."

I clench my jaw against the surge of desire welling in me. He's not wrong. If he pushed just a little harder, we'd be fucking on the desk in no time at all. And I'd be loving every minute of it. Until it was over, anyway. After which I'd be kicking myself for more or less sleeping with the enemy. It was different when I didn't know that that's who he was.

But he backs off, stepping away and going to his side of the desk. He puts his hands on the back of his desk chair, and we stare at each other for a minute. I'd break the silence, but I have no clue what to say. For once.

"I don't mean to push," he finally says. "But I'm not going anywhere. And you'll see. Just give me more time, and you'll understand."

I shake my head, snapping myself out of the trance he's had me in. He doesn't know me at all. He doesn't know where I come from, what my life is like. Someone like him could never understand my world. So while I am obviously still very attracted to him, no amount of time can change our fundamental differences.

But hopefully, if nothing else, whatever he's got planned for the cardiac unit, and Rutherford Hospital, will start to make sense. And maybe it'll even all be okay. Then I can get back to my life, sans Noah Rutherford.

# CHAPTER 11

I spend Sunday morning at the nursing home, trying not to worry about my father's now raging lung infection that isn't responding well to antibiotics. Aspiration pneumonia looms in his future, and I know I'm just going to work myself into hysterics if I think too much about it. Or about my mother's increasingly frail frame. Their respective degenerative diseases are eating away at the strong, loving people I once knew.

And my finances, for that matter. But I try not to discuss any of that while I'm there, with Katie or otherwise. All I can do is what's in my power and let go of the rest. It's certainly a constant battle when I'm not at work, when I'm not so busy there's no time to think.

But as I head out of the city a half hour ahead of my scheduled hot air balloon tour, the excitement overrides it all, and the only thing I can think about is soaring among the clouds, feeling free for once in my life.

I follow the directions I was given to an address along the coast, just west of the Del Mar Fairgrounds. Driving down the road toward my destination, I can already spot a striped red-and-white domed top that must be the hot air balloon. Excitement unfurls in my stomach. And maybe a bit of nerves too.

# YOU CAN'T BUY LOVE

I pull into a driveway with a heavy iron gate that sits open and drive down the narrow road. It ends in a large, circular parking lot with a large storage shed on the south side. I park just inside the circle, on the easternmost edge. A vast field surrounds me as I step out of the car.

The only other vehicle there is a Range Rover, parked on the westernmost side of the circle. Beyond that, I can see the balloon. I let out a snort, realizing I should have known that one of Mr. Rutherford's rich friends owned the balloon and donated rides for all their stuck-up jerk friends. In fact, I bet they own this whole parcel of land. Prime freaking waterfront real estate just outside of San Diego proper for their luxurious little hobby.

Lord, I hope I'm not about to spend three hours with the most pretentious asshat on the planet. With a sigh, I resign myself to whatever I'll have to endure to do this. Because like hell I'm passing up this opportunity.

Equal parts guarded and eager, I approach. But as I get closer, I don't see *anyone.* Just the large, high-sided woven brown square basket that looks like it could comfortably hold six people, and the massive balloon hovering over it. Thick ropes clearly bolted into the ground are attached to pegs on the corners of the basket, holding it to the earth.

I stand about twenty feet away, unsure of what to do, realizing I never got a name or a phone number for the ride operator.

"Hello?" I call out nervously.

A man pops up from inside the basket, holding a wrench in his hand. Well, that explains that. A loud noise above him startles me, drawing my attention up to the mechanism in the balloon's opening that is now spewing fire, presumably to keep the balloon properly inflated.

When my eyes drift back down, the man has moved toward me. And if I was startled a second ago, now I'm just shocked. And pissed off.

"What the fuck are *you* doing here?" I snap as Noah approaches.

He grins, rubbing his hands on a dirty rag as he takes in my fitted jeans and green T-shirt.

"She's mine," he replies, gesturing toward the balloon. "And it's nice to see you too, Julianna."

I cross my arms over my chest. "I should've known," I grumble, shaking my head. "Any particular reason you didn't bother mentioning that you *owned* the damn hot air balloon trip I was bidding on?" I scoff internally, adding it to the list of things he conveniently forgot to tell me that night.

He tucks the rag in his back pocket, stopping in front of me. "I don't usually start conversations with, 'Hi, I'm Noah Rutherford. Would you like to take a ride in my hot air balloon?'" he replies.

I raise an eyebrow, willing myself not to laugh at him mocking himself. "Really? It seems like that's exactly the kind of thing that would impress the kind of woman you'd want to be with," I retort.

"Oh, ye of little faith," he says with a smile, shaking his head. "Does that mean you're not interested in going up?"

My throat constricts at the idea of not going.

"Can you really fly this thing?" I ask, not even sure if I really want to be trapped with him. Because he looks so casual in his old, faded jeans and white tee. So happy. So *hot*. I'm only human, after all, but I don't want to be tricked into falling for his charms. Into forgetting what he's done, and may still do.

"Yes. I'm licensed, insured, and have been doing this for the better part of twenty years, Julianna. You have nothing to worry about."

He sounds and looks so confident that it's difficult *not* to believe him. About this, at least. And I realize I want to believe him. Maybe it's just because this is one of the things I've wanted to do for a long time, but what the hell. Which makes me realize something.

"You didn't make this the 'gimme' prize after the fact just so you could get me alone, did you?" I ask suspiciously.

Noah tips his head back and laughs. "No, but that would've been pretty smooth, wouldn't it?" he teases.

I glare at him, unconvinced. "Or incredibly presumptuous and creepy."

I hear the rumble of a vehicle behind me and turn to see a large truck pulling a trailer parking next to the Range Rover. Two men jump out, bringing a couple of bags with them as they approach.

"Julianna, this is my ground crew," Noah explains as the men join us. "John," he gestures to the older of the two, "and Robbie." Both have the same dark hair, eyes, and complexion. I suspect they are father and son.

They greet me politely, and the three of them confer over whatever it is they brought back, making some adjustments and doing their thing. Not long later, Noah comes back to me.

"She's ready. So what'll it be, Julianna? I promise I won't bite," he teases, hands on hips, a challenging smile on his full lips.

I lift my chin. "I'm not scared of you, Noah," I reply firmly. The words have more meaning than I intended them to. Though on second thought, that might not have been an accident.

But his smile widens regardless. "That's my girl," he replies. "Come on."

I don't even have time to react to his words before he's pulling me by the hand toward the basket. John takes a moment to give me a few simple instructions — basic stuff like don't lean over the basket in the air, don't touch anything, and stay out of Noah's way if there's an emergency. As he talks, Noah climbs into the basket. Then it's my turn.

I mount the stepladder and let Noah help me ease down into the basket. Even just holding his hand in that small moment sends my stomach flip-flopping.

And before I know it, the ropes are untied, and the burner, as it's aptly named, is firing the air in the balloon up so we're lifting gently into the sky. There's little time for talk as Noah finishes communicating with the ground crew and navigates us over the treetops. As we rise, more of the land and ocean around us becomes visible, and my excitement spills over.

Suddenly, I understand the temptation to lean over the side, but I resist. It's not like I can't see everything anyway. Little is obscured by the four ropes tying the basket to the balloon, and I barely feel the slow drift as we rise. It's almost like being in a tall building. Well, unless you look down. I try that once and only once before keeping my eyes trained on the horizon, which seems endless.

Tears fill my eyes and I feel Noah next to me. I look up to find him smiling down at me.

"Beautiful, isn't it?" he asks softly.

I nod, unable to form words. In the late afternoon sunshine, the clear skies are gorgeous, the views of the water, the downtown skyline in the distance, and all of the other visible landmarks beyond stunning. It's even better than I thought it would be. Floating through the air like we're celestial beings, separate from everything below us while we look down on it as if it's all part of a diorama. It's surreal.

After a few minutes of staring in awe, I look back up at Noah.

"I see the draw," I admit. "It's a beautiful escape, Noah, thank you."

If I had endless amounts of cash, I'd probably own one of these too. But that part I don't admit out loud.

Noah lifts a camera I hadn't noticed he was holding, silently asking permission. I nod and put on my best impression of a smile as he takes a few pictures of me and the views around us. When he lowers the camera, he looks at me carefully.

"What are you escaping from?" he asks simply.

I snort. "What are *you* escaping from?" I return, unwilling to be the first to offer anything personal.

He gives an understanding smile that doesn't reach his eyes.

"Is it weird that I use something my family's privilege gave me to escape *being* a Rutherford, if only for a little while?" he muses.

"That's not weird," I admit, for the first time considering that Noah didn't choose to be who he is. "Why work for your dad, then, if that's something you need to escape from?"

"Oh, it's not work that's the problem," he clarifies. "If it were, I would've done what my little sister did and gotten into something totally unrelated to the family business. No, I actually love the job. It's the name. Sometimes it opens

doors, but most of the time it just puts people's guards up."
He looks at me pointedly.

"Well, I'm sure the doors it opens are worth the ones it closes," I reply drily, looking away.

"True," he replies thoughtfully. "It did help me raise millions for Alzheimer's research. Thanks to generous donations like yours."

I look back at him in shock, and he winks at me.

"*You* picked the Alzheimer's Foundation of America?" I gasp.

"I did. Is there a problem with that?" he asks with a frown.

"No, I just … why?"

In stark opposition to his usual confidence, he shifts uncomfortably. "My nan," he finally says by way of explanation, looking away. "It was the least I could do, after everything she did for me."

My heart breaks for him. He chose it because he knows what it's like to watch someone he loves suffer from it. I reach out and take his hand.

"Hey," I say, getting him to meet my eyes. "I understand how powerless you feel. But I'm impressed that you used the power you have to do something about it."

"Do you?" he asks, looking so forlorn I want to wrap him in my arms.

I close my eyes and sigh. "I do. My father has it too."

Before I can even open my eyes again, he's pulled me into his arms. I think about resisting for a moment, but it just feels too good. I lean into him, and he rests his chin on the top of my head.

"How's he doing?" Noah murmurs.

"Not good. He's eighty and has had it for about ten years. He's got a lung infection now, and I'm afraid he's not going to be able to fight it much longer." I stop, unable to say anything else without losing composure. I take a deep breath to steady myself before pulling away.

As I pull back, his hand sweeps down my arm, then squeezes my palm gently.

"I'm so sorry, Julianna, I had no idea," he replies.

I shrug, withdrawing my hand. "Wouldn't be so bad if my mother didn't start suffering from dementia a few years back too," I respond. "Seeing both of them like this ... it's rough. So I understand is all. How's your nan?"

Noah looks at me with pity written all over his face, and it cuts through me, self-consciousness crawling across my skin.

"She had other issues that were more pressing," he finally replies, thankfully not offering any words of sympathy for my family's situation, "but the hardest part was watching her go through it all without the ability to remember what was happening to her. It made everything so much worse. She passed away a few years ago, though, so her fight is over. But I'll do everything in my power to help others avoid going through that. To avoid having to watch loved ones go through it."

The heaviness of his declaration, of the thoughts I usually keep at bay with busyness, it all sits like a boulder on my chest, making it difficult to breathe. I turn away, needing to focus on my surroundings, the beauty that we're floating through.

"Shouldn't you be steering or something?" I ask abruptly.

I feel Noah's heat behind me. His smell invades my senses. It simultaneously makes me angry and ... well, other things I'm not ready to admit to.

"The wind has us, Julianna. I'm just here to make sure you stay safe," he says quietly. "There's still a bit until sunset. Are you hungry?"

I blink away tears I hadn't realized were there and turn to him with a forced smile.

"Sure, what have you got?"

He unearths a picnic basket that had been tucked into the corner. It's filled with champagne, crackers, cheese, and cookies. Not exactly a well-rounded dinner, but it's all delicious and indulgent, so I can hardly complain.

While we eat, he tells me about his little sister and her career as an artist. How angry that made his dad, and how much his nan used to laugh over it all. It makes me ache with memories of my parents when we would all laugh and joke and … well, love.

Watching Noah talk about his family is also very revealing. He loves them all, clearly, but is obviously often at odds with his father. It makes me wonder why he chose to work so closely with him. Surely, given his education, experience, and name, he could work anywhere. But I don't ask. I already feel like I'm softening toward him too much. I don't want to dig that hole deeper. Because after this is over, he still has my career, and the careers of everyone I care about, in his hands. Hands I'm still not entirely sure I can trust.

As it is, the sunset almost does me in. While we drift back to earth, the glowing orb dips below the horizon, lacing oranges and pinks into the dimming sky, then deepening to purples as the ground gets closer and closer.

While we're still hovering over the treetops, and after Noah has radioed his ground crew, I feel his eyes on me. I look up and give him a smile.

"This was better than anything I could've imagined," I assure him. "Thank you."

"You deserve it," he says huskily, drawing a little too close for comfort. His hands come to my shoulders, and I swallow hard. "And so much more."

I make to pull back, but his fingers hold me firmly in place. He studies my face for a moment, and I have to force myself to breathe. And to not give in to the sultry look he's giving me. I stay as still as possible. But then, I think to myself, *He's not a T-rex, Jules — staying still isn't going to make it so he can't see you.* And laughter bubbles out of me.

"What's so funny?" he asks, his lips pulling up into a smile.

I shake my head and press my lips together, thankful that I managed to disrupt the moment. I pull out of his embrace. "Nothing, just a silly thought. So how do you land a hot air balloon?"

Taking the hint, he steps back.

"Well, see, that's the thing," he says. "The hot air balloon kind of lands you." He gives me a wink and picks up his radio. He either doesn't see or chooses to ignore the nervous look I shoot him.

But as it happens, there was nothing to worry about. Despite seeming awfully close to some trees, we land pretty cleanly in a grassy area. It's not long before the truck appears, with the Range Rover on its tail. John climbs out of the truck, Robbie out of the Range Rover. They work to help Noah secure the basket.

Noah climbs out first, then helps me out. Robbie hands Noah his keys.

"They'll handle the teardown," Noah assures me. "I'll drive you back to your car."

I guess I hadn't thought too much about the fact that hot air balloons don't land where they took off, or that that meant after several hours of being together in the balloon we'd need to spend more time alone in a car. Without the majestic views to distract us.

But I don't have much choice, so I go with him, trying not to notice how ridiculously luxurious the leather interior is. Or how good he looks leaned back in his seat, one arm draped casually over the steering wheel. I stay silent, not trusting myself to engage further after the forced intimacy of the evening.

When we finally pull up to the original meeting spot, next to my car, Noah cuts the engine and looks at me.

"I hope you enjoyed yourself," he says.

"I did, thank you," I reply simply.

"Good. And I hate to end this evening on a sour note, but I want you to hear this from me. Since last time didn't go so well."

My heart jumps into my throat. "You're firing someone else," I realize. God, I'm so stupid. Of course he is. Of course he was playing nice all evening, building up my trust for exactly this moment. I steel myself, wiping my expression blank, not wanting to give him the satisfaction of any kind of response. "All right then. Who?"

He shakes his head and splays his hands out.

"It's not one person, Julianna. We're going to be letting go somewhere around a quarter of the hospital's staff," he admits.

My heart starts hammering in my ears as blind rage threatens to overtake me. It takes every ounce of self-control that I possess not to let it out.

"If you're trying to get me to trust you, tricking me into a hot air balloon ride with you, then ending it by telling me you're going to be firing a bunch of my friends isn't exactly the way to go about it," I finally say tightly.

The look he gives me is filled with fire and fury.

"You bid on the damn prize," he replies hotly. "I didn't trick you into anything. And yes, it's shit luck that this happened at the same time, but would you rather have found out with everyone else at work tomorrow? Because I thought hearing it from me, honestly and beforehand, would show you that I'm not trying to blindside you."

I throw up my hands. "I meant for you to take what I've said into consideration. To trust me. To involve me in these kinds of things. Not just give me the heads up when you're about to drop the ax. What difference does it make? There's nothing I can do about it now."

He slams a hand on the steering wheel in an uncharacteristic display of anger. "Dammit, I did listen to you. But in the end, it's not totally up to me. This was just decided Friday, so it's not like I had a lot of time to tell you. And if I'm being totally honest, you're not even meant to know."

"Great, so, what, I'm supposed to be thankful you told me anyway? Even though it's completely what the hospital *doesn't* need and there's nothing I can do about it? Thanks for keeping me in the loop," I shoot back in disgust.

He glares daggers at me, making me even angrier. "Did it ever occur to you that you may not know *everything*? That you may not be the best person to decide what the hospital does and doesn't need?" he retorts.

"It doesn't matter now," I mumble. "I should get home. Sounds like I'm going to need to be well-rested to deal with the shitstorm tomorrow." I make to get out of the car, but he grabs my arm.

"Julianna, wait, I don't want to leave things like this," he pleads.

I pull my arm away and climb out of the car. "There's nothing to leave. This is the way things are, Noah," I shoot back over my shoulder. I slam the door behind me, climbing into my car and getting the hell out of there before he can stop me.

I angrily replay the whole scene over and over on the drive home. By the time I climb into bed, I'm far too pissed off to sleep. So I toss and turn for hours, knowing that my lack of sleep is going to make this so much worse. Not that all the sleep in the world will change what's about to happen.

# CHAPTER 12

Monday is every bit as hard as I thought it would be. I'm an absolute mess: exhausted, angry, and surly in a way that I never am. I'm usually the positive one in tough times, the one to assure everyone else that everything will be okay, that we'll make it work, figure it out.

But when MacDougall announces that some of the staff will be let go in the coming days, despite everyone's clear panic, I don't have it in me to put on a brave face and reassure them. How can I when I know exactly how deep they plan to cut our already overworked staff?

I shut out even Sasha when she asks what I know, unwilling to talk about Noah Rutherford. Even *thinking* his name makes me angry.

But on Tuesday, when they let the first ten percent go, I realize I have only myself to blame for bringing attention to the hospital. I'm the one who told Noah about the problems here that made him want to look closer.

This round we only lost Harper. Becca, Sasha, and everyone else are understandably heartbroken. She was the last non-doctor hired, though, so I'm not surprised. And I'm also heartbroken, but in a totally different way. The disappointment I feel is all with myself. And in knowing there's nothing I can do to stop this.

Though midweek, I wonder if there is.

Tail between my legs, I go to Noah's office, thinking I might be able to make a case to keep the rest. Maybe I can get him to listen.

But he won't even see me.

And that's when the anger starts again.

I'm storming toward MacDougall's office to give him a piece of my mind instead when a voice stops me.

"Whoa there, Jules," comes Cal's lilting British accent.

I whirl on the spot to face him peeking out of his office door. He holds up his hands in an obvious "I come in peace" gesture, but it doesn't make me any less pissed off.

"What?" I snap.

"Given the look on your face and the direction you're heading, I think maybe you and I should have a little chat before you do something ill advised," he suggests gently.

"What good would that do?" I huff, crossing my arms over my chest.

His eyebrows shoot up. "Well, probably a whole hell of a lot more good than having a go at the chief of the cardiac unit," he replies patiently.

I furrow my brow and frown. The man has a point.

"Fine," I reply, following him into his office.

He sits back in his chair, and I slump into the one in front of his desk.

"So, care to tell me what has you in a strop?" he asks.

"Oh, I don't know, maybe the fact that they've just fired a bunch of people and are about to fire more even though we're stretched thin as it is?" I snap.

"Mmm," he hums. "Are you sure that's what's really bothering you?" He gives me a knowing look. And it hits me.

"Sasha *told you*?" I say accusatorily.

His brows pull together. "I'm afraid I don't know what you're referring to," he replies, and I don't hear any dishonesty in his words. "I was speaking of the fact that you've been walking around in a mood ever since Noah Rutherford joined us a couple of weeks ago. So I presumed you had some sort of previous issue with him that's really fueling all this rage."

I snort. "You could say that."

He raises an eyebrow. "So this isn't really just about the firings, is it?" he prompts.

I fold my arms over my chest. "No, I suppose not."

"What's it about, then, Jules? You're always so levelheaded. I've never seen you like this, and I find it rather disconcerting. Please, tell me, I'd like to be able to help if I can," he prompts gently.

I heave a deep sigh and rub my eyes. "I met Noah Rutherford at the charity gala last month. Except, I didn't know who he was, and I …" I chew on my lip self-consciously, not sure how to put this. "I may have shared my concerns about the hospital with him."

Cal steeples his fingers under his nose and thinks about that for a moment. Then his crystal-clear blue eyes look up to meet mine.

"You think this is all your fault," he deduces.

"Yes," I breathe. "No. I don't know. Maybe. If I hadn't said anything, he wouldn't be here. So yeah, I guess, in a way, I think this is my fault. For a while I thought he might listen to me and really understand where the problems are coming from. But it seems I was wrong." I shake my head, the anger seeping out of me as despair takes over.

Cal leans forward, placing his elbows on his desk and spearing me with a hard look.

"I hate to break it to you, but if this is anyone's fault, it's mine," he replies.

"You've only been here six months, how is any of this your fault?" I ask tiredly.

He blows out a breath and leans back in his chair. "The thing is, you've worked at Rutherford Hospital your entire career, am I correct?" he asks.

I tilt my head, unsure of where he's going with his question. "I had a job at one other hospital before Rutherford, but it was less than a year. So basically, yes."

"Through my training and career I've now worked at …" he pauses, squinting as if he's trying to do the mental math. "Eight different hospitals in the last ten years. So I've got quite a lot more to compare it to than you do." The arrogant edge to his tone makes me bristle, but he's usually got a point when he gets like this, so I let him continue. "At every single one of those hospitals, the nurses always say they're understaffed and overworked. Do you know why?"

I roll my eyes. "Because it's a universal problem that hospital administrators don't understand how much nurses actually do?" I scoff.

Cal huffs an unamused chuckle. "No, Jules. I know it feels like that. But it's because you do a damn hard job. And shorter shifts and more people aren't going to change that. Your shifts aren't designed for your comfort, they're designed to keep the hospital running smoothly for the patients. That's not to say there aren't times when we are, in fact, understaffed, because good medical personnel are hard to come by. And I'm afraid much of Rutherford's staff isn't up to standard, which is contributing to your feeling that we're unable to handle everything that needs doing."

"You told your bosses all of this, didn't you?" I gasp. "*That's* why they're letting people go."

"Julianna," he says with a caution in his voice. "I think we both need to stop thinking about this situation as if one person is responsible. Yours was the voice that raised the red flag. Mine was another voice that added to the picture. Hell, even Dr. MacDougall is a small player in everything that's happening. There is a hospital full of opinions, piles of data, and all of the Rutherford Group's staff and experience behind the actions that are being taken here. So your anger is for naught. It's difficult, I know. Change always is. But nothing you can say to MacDougall will help. In fact, all it's likely to do is land you in hot water."

I look up at the ceiling and blink back tears.

"God, Cal, I hate it when you have a point," I say, my voice thick with emotion. Once I've mastered myself, I look back down at him.

"I know," he replies with a wink. "Feel better now?"

I shake my head. "Not really. But you're right, mouthing off to MacDougall is just going to make things worse. Thanks for talking me off the ledge."

"Anytime," he replies, rising from his desk. "Now, I'm sure I'm supposed to be somewhere right now."

I smile. "Yeah, probably me too."

He pats me genially on the back and we both go about our business. But I wasn't lying. I really don't feel better, because I've realized my only options seem to be to just deal with it … or leave. And somehow I still can't help feeling like Noah is the problem here. That he's still talking out both sides of his mouth by trying to keep me happy yet still enact all the harsh changes that are being handed down. Because it can't be both.

\* \* \*

The week marches on despite everything, but when Becca comes back from her lunch break on Friday, she looks like she's going to be sick.

"You okay, Becks?" Sasha asks quietly, jumping up and rubbing her back gently.

Becca fixes her with a sad look and shakes her head. I set down the patient file I'd just retrieved for my next appointment and round the nurses' station counter.

"Hey, what happened?" I ask.

Becca looks up at me with tears in her eyes, and my stomach drops. I can't remember ever seeing Becca cry. She's such a tough cookie, and usually a master at hiding her more vulnerable moments.

"They just fired Vincent," she whispers.

"No!" Sasha and I both exclaim at the same time.

"Those bastards," Sasha adds.

"I'm so sorry," I say.

"He didn't deserve it. He's been through too damn much," Becca snaps, angrily wiping at her eyes.

"It's not going to mess up anything for him, is it?" Sasha asks, knowing Vincent is still dealing with the legal fallout of what he and Becca went through with his ex last month.

"No, he's got time to figure something out before it becomes a problem," she assures us. "He's just been so … happy. This really hit him hard."

I pull her into a hug. "It's tough seeing the people you care about upset," I respond, even though I'm talking about me and her. But it applies to us all at the moment, really.

Becca gives me a squeeze then lets me go. "Yeah. I know we'll get through it. It just sucks is all. Thanks for listening, bitches," she says.

We all laugh a little. Trust Becca to lighten the mood, even when she's the one who's upset.

"You know we're always here for you," I tell her.

She nods.

"Except right now, you're supposed to be in exam six," Sasha points out with a small smile.

"Okay, fine, except right this exact second," I agree with a chuckle. "You gonna be okay?"

"Yeah, I'm fine, Jules, thanks," Becca assures me.

As I walk away, I can hear Sasha continuing to console and commiserate with Becca. And the day's not over yet. I know there will probably be at least one person to go from our unit too. So I can't help the feeling of dread that sticks with me as I go about my duties.

The afternoon flies by and, before I know it, Sarah shows up as I'm returning an EKG machine to the supply closet.

"Holy crap, is it already five-thirty?" I ask as I close the closet door and return to the nurses' station.

"Yep. How'd it go today? Who got the ax?" Sarah asks bluntly.

I shake my head. "Becca's boyfriend over in intensive care. Randi up in maternity. Nobody from cardiac," I reply. I open my mouth to continue the list, but as if I cursed it, MacDougall comes down the hall looking stern.

"Nurse Marcus, I'd like a word with you in my office, please," he says in a condescending tone.

Eyes wide, I look at her in horror. She shakes her head, clearly already having realized we weren't out of the woods yet.

As I go about finishing my end-of-shift rounds, my stomach is all in knots. Thankfully, when I return to the nurses' station right at six, Sarah is already back, though looking grim.

"They're killing second shift and going to an on-call model," she says before I can ask. "I've been offered a position in oncology. Zoe will move back to day shift."

"Well, shit. That's definitely going to make things tough around here. Though it could've been worse. At least they didn't fire anyone, right?" I prompt.

She shrugs but stays silent. As she makes for the supply cabinets behind the desk, something about her posture, her attitude, doesn't sit right with me.

"What else happened?" I press.

She turns and looks me squarely in the eye. "Sasha will be promoted to ARNP in my stead. She'll train under you."

My insides jump a little with happiness. *Finally*, they're going to promote Sasha. But I give Sarah a funny look. "And that's a bad thing because …?"

"Because I wasn't even given the option to stay in cardiac and have Sasha move. It just doesn't seem fair. This whole thing stinks of favoritism," she seethes.

"Well, technically, Sasha's worked here longer than you," I point out. "Granted, not in an ARNP role, but still."

Boy, was that the wrong thing to say. I can practically feel Sarah's anger as she abruptly turns her back to me and fishes around in the cabinets.

"That's not how seniority works around here, and you know it," she snaps. She turns back toward me with an armload of empty bins. "But then, I'm not fucking Noah Rutherford, so I guess I don't get a say in any of these decisions."

My jaw drops and her eyes narrow.

"Don't even deny it, Jules. Of all people, I never thought *you* would stab me in the back," she says hotly.

"I … who did you …" I stutter, unable to get out a coherent sentence. But she doesn't give me a chance, storming past me.

"I don't want to hear it. Just go. Your shift is over anyway."

And then she's gone. I stand there, completely flabbergasted. Sasha and Becca are the only ones who know, and I trust them both. Even Becca, despite her gossipy tendencies, because she's practically like a sister to me, and I know she'd never betray my confidence.

So the only way Sarah could know is if the information didn't come from me, Sasha, or Becca.

Noah. Noah told someone here.

And now the rumor mill knows.

Fury rips through me. After all he's done, all he's doing, adding this to the pile tips me over the edge. I'm over taking this bullshit from him. I don't care if he fires me on the spot, he's going to hear exactly what I think of all the changes he's handing down. Hell, even better if he does. Then at least he won't have completely ruined my reputation. Because he's already ruining where I work and the lives of people I care about.

I know the bastard is still here, and it's time to let him have it.

# CHAPTER 13

It takes all of my strength not to bang on Noah's office door like I'm trying to break it down. Even though I feel like doing exactly that, which causes me to knock a little more forcefully than I'd intended.

When the door swings open in my face, I jump back in surprise. Noah looks equally surprised — and unhappy — to see me, though he recovers quickly.

"Come in and sit," he barks, stepping back.

I enter and he closes the door behind me, but rather than sit down, I whirl on him.

"Don't *ever* come banging on my door like that," he snaps, beating me to the punch. "Now *sit down*."

"I'm done taking orders from you," I retort. "How *could you*, Noah? Better yet, *why*? Does it make you feel like a big man for everyone to know you've fucked me? That if you can conquer Julianna Magnusson, everyone else should suck your cock too?"

A look of shock passes over his face before it's replaced by anger. "I haven't told a soul," he swears. "Is that why you came in here flying off the handle?"

"Oh, you haven't even begun to see me fly off the fucking handle," I promise in a low voice. "If you didn't tell anyone, who did then? And even if you deny that, you can't deny that you promoted Sasha at Sarah's expense. How do you think that made me look?"

He advances on me, causing me to take steps backward. "I can't do what you ask, you're angry," he seethes. "I try to do something else you asked for instead and you're angry. What do you want from me, Julianna?"

As the back of my legs hit the desk, he stops advancing. But now I'm pinned, and it doesn't help my anger any.

"Why does the rumor mill know we slept together?" I insist, ignoring his other statements.

"I don't know," he insists tightly. "Does it even matter?"

I look up into his eyes, their normal honeyed brown shade a hard amber.

"It matters to me. When this is all over, you'll go back to your ivory tower. But I'll still have to deal with the reputation of having fucked Noah Rutherford in exchange for … well, anything they feel like chalking up to me being your plaything. You may be untouchable, but *I'm not*. None of this would have ever happened if you'd just told me who you were."

I choke on a sob. And it makes me realize what I'm experiencing is so much worse than anger. There's emotion here. Feelings. Ones I don't want to have right now.

His expression softens, and it makes it even worse. He reaches up and cups my cheek in his hand. "You've never been a plaything to me," he says on a sigh. "And I honestly don't know how they found out. But I can't undo that. And I wouldn't, in a million years, undo our night together either."

He eyes my lips like a starved man, and my insides tighten. I close my eyes, and I'm torn between my logical brain, screaming all its anger, all its objections that he's the enemy, and the memories that his smell and his closeness evoke, causing a physical response I'm having trouble controlling.

His thumb brushes over my bottom lip. "This week has been rough for me too. And I've wanted to come to you a million times," he admits. "But I didn't want to push you away either. Seems like that was inevitable, though. But fuck if I wish it weren't."

I open my eyes and look up into his. And all logic flies out the window. All I want is his lips. I *need* his lips. His hands. His body. I hate that I do. But right now, I want to wipe away everything. Forget everything. And the only time I can remember being able to do that was with him inside me.

It stirs so many emotions. Anger comes back to the forefront. One minute I want to rage at him, to make him pay for the hurt he's had a hand in causing. The next I want him to take it all off my mind with his body. How thin the line between love and hate is.

I put a hand to his chest as the lust battles with my anger.

Then I hear someone walking down the hall just outside his office door. And it brings me fully back to my senses.

It's time to put a stop to whatever this moment might have been. Because it won't undo any of the hurt. Not really.

"It's not just what you're doing, it's also who you are," I explain. "So yes, it was inevitable."

He takes a step back, letting out a breath. He looks so defeated, so tired, that I know he wasn't lying about this being hard on him too.

I equally care and don't.

In any case, I'm too exhausted for any of this now that the fight has gone out of me.

"For what it's worth, I'm sorry," he says quietly. "I never wanted to hurt you. I'm not sure what I can do about the rumor mill, but I will see what I can do to make things right with Nurse Marcus. That may mean your friend will be moved to another department, though."

I nod my understanding, knowing he's not the kind of man who apologizes easily. It adds to my confusion, to the ball of emotions swirling inside me.

"Thank you."

I don't dare look at him. I simply slip past him, heading for the door.

"Julianna?" he calls after me.

I stop, hand on the doorknob, and chance a look back. He has his hands shoved in his pockets, his expression defeated.

"I can't change who I am. So if it's that much of an issue …" He shakes his head. "Well, I guess I'll have to accept that that's where you're at."

"Good," I say tightly, even though his words still hurt. "I guess we can both move on now."

His jaw tightens. "If that's what you want."

I nod. "That's what I want."

After that, I don't give him the chance to make this harder, and I leave.

I beat myself up the whole way home. For what, I'm not sure. I'm so confused and I don't know what to think.

Well, I know one thing. Things aren't going to get any easier at Rutherford Hospital in the near future. So now might be a good time to explore my options.

Time to dust off my résumé.

\* \* \*

"Seriously? You're just going to switch jobs? Just like that?" Katie's expression is skeptical.

I don't blame her. Even I'm having a hard time wrapping my head around it.

"Not 'just like that,'" I reply, using my fingers as air quotes. "But I don't think it would be a bad idea to have an out."

Katie shakes her head. "If you say so, but it sounds an awful lot like running from your problems to me," she responds.

"Even after working there all this time, spending years building up a reputation of trust and integrity, one stupid rumor and they all think I'm whoring myself out for my friends," I point out, shaking my head. "And who knows what else the Rutherfords have planned for us. Seriously, Katie, I'd be an idiot not to be thinking about a Plan B."

"You're not an idiot, Jules. Not if you stay or if you go. And not even if you do secretly have the hots for Noah Rutherford," she replies airily.

I roll my eyes. Only Katie can see right through me. "Fine, I have … urges when he's around. But I'm a grown woman. I'll manage."

"Well, I hope you do more than manage," she responds. "I hope you jump that —"

I put my hands over my ears. "Lalalalala," I sing. I see Katie's mouth close into a smirk, so I drop my hands. "Subject change, please."

"Oh, good, because I have news," she says.

"That you waited until now to mention?" I ask incredulously.

She waves a hand dismissively. "You needed to vent. Anyway. You remember that drug trial for Alzheimer's patients with lung infections?"

YOU CAN'T BUY LOVE

"Yeah, the one we tried to get him in the first time this happened," I recall, my face falling. Dad's lungs keep getting worse, though they haven't officially declared it aspiration pneumonia yet. "Why?"

"Well, he's in," she says simply.

My mouth pops open. "Really? Did we reapply?"

Katie shrugs. "I guess they kept his file open, since they have access to his status in the system. Any which way, they said they had an opening for him now."

"Oh, thank god," I say, breathing a sigh of relief. "When can they start him?"

The drug in question has had a high success rate of not only eliminating infection but also improving lung functionality afterward. It will mean less suffering overall and less risk going forward.

Katie grins. "I gave him his first dose yesterday. He gets another after lunch today. Shall we?" She gestures to the kitchen, and I happily follow. As we work, she fills me in on the details of the program. Not only are they providing the drug for free, but they'll also be paying for all of his medical expenses. So all I need to pay now is the room and board for keeping him in the home. Which, frankly, was the cheapest part of this whole arrangement, so it's an unexpected and very pleasant surprise. Finally, some good news.

* * *

Unfortunately, when I return to work on Monday, my gossip spidey-senses start tingling immediately. Something in the air just feels off. I stop at the help desk to find Melinda, the morning shift receptionist, practically vibrating out of her seat with excitement.

"Morning, Jules," she chirps.

"Hey, Melinda, nice weekend?" I ask, knowing she needs the small talk to warm up.

"Oh, it was great," she gushes. "Hal and I went out on the boat with some friends. How about you?"

"My dad got into a drug trial for his lung infection, so things are looking up, thanks," I reply with a forced smile. I just wanted to shake her and ask her to spill it already.

"That's wonderful, I'm so happy to hear that," she replies. "So have you heard yet?"

Fucking finally.

"Heard what?" I ask innocently.

She giggles. "You know that sexy Mr. Rutherford who's been here the last few weeks?" she whispers loudly. Why she bothers, I don't know, because you could still hear her all the way up in neurology on the top floor with that tone. And there's no way in hell she didn't hear the rumor about me and Noah, so I'm pretty sure she already knows that I'm well aware of him, to say the least.

"What about him?" I ask, playing along, eyes wide in feigned excitement.

"There are pictures of him all over the gossip sites this morning," she says. "With a *movie star*."

My eyebrows jump, and I'm not pretending to be interested now.

"Show me," I demand sharply, ever the masochist.

Melinda happily taps away at her computer and turns the screen toward me. Sure enough, there's Noah. In all his gorgeous glory, wearing a charcoal suit, headed into one of the nicest restaurants in town with the gorgeous blond Piper Black, a young, popular film actress who's so hot right now even I've heard of her. She clings happily to Noah's arm, positively oozing sex appeal in a tight black dress that leaves absolutely nothing to the imagination.

My stomach turns, the carafe of coffee I called breakfast threatening to make a reappearance.

And I realize suddenly that Melinda is watching me. Or watching my reaction, as it were. Shit. She definitely knew. Still, I manage a feeble smile.

"Was that over the weekend?" I ask quietly.

She nods. "Saturday night," she confirms.

"Well, isn't that something?" I murmur. Guess he moved on pretty damn fast. Clearly, our night together didn't mean that much. Though he was probably only acting like it did so he could get a replay in his office. I suddenly feel like I'm going to be ill again.

Melinda gives me a feline grin, clearly noting and enjoying my discomfort.

"Guess he's more like his brother than we knew," she comments with an affected shrug.

I force a small laugh, but it sounds pathetic even to me.

"Guess so. Anyway, best be getting to it. Have a great day, Melinda," I reply.

"You too," she calls to my retreating back.

A shot of disgust rolls through me. Because Piper Black is exactly the kind of woman I'd imagine someone like Noah with. I was an idiot for thinking I could ever hold the interest of a man like him. Which is fine, because I didn't want to anyway … right?

The rest of the day is awkward as ass. Even Sasha and Becca give me a wide berth, believing me to be the woman scorned. I don't say anything to anyone about any of it. I'm not breathing life into any of this gossip. I just want it all to be over.

By the end of the week, the rumor mill has decided I'm the victim in this situation. Just another woman used up by another philandering Rutherford playboy. It should be a welcome turn of events, but the whole thing has just made me sick to my stomach.

So when a private cardiologist's office contacts me on Thursday for a Sunday interview, I happily accept. It was the one job in a sea of listings where I actually knew someone who'd worked there and could recommend me. I was starting to worry the job market was too cutthroat right now, so the in saved me. Because it's time to start lining up Plan B, since things sure as hell aren't getting any better around here.

# CHAPTER 14

The job interview with Dr. Foster, the private cardiologist, goes well. So well, in fact, that he tells me on the spot that he's ready to extend me an offer whenever I'm ready to leave Rutherford Hospital, assuming that's in the next few weeks.

I should feel better having solidified my Plan B. But all I feel is more pressure to make a decision.

But Wednesday brings a development that firmly shoves me over the edge.

Becca gets called into MacDougall's office at the end of the day. She returns not five minutes later, pale and shaking.

"I've been fired," she says plainly.

Sasha and I both stare in shocked silence.

"You've … been fired?" Sasha asks haltingly.

Becca nods, gathering her things from behind the desk while blinking back tears.

"For what?" I demand.

Becca shrugs. "Part of the cutbacks. What else?" she says. She's keeping her words short, but I can tell how upset she is.

I grab the purse out of her hands and set it on the desk.

"Come with me," I direct, grabbing her by the elbow and marching down the hall to MacDougall's office.

I rap my knuckles on the door but don't wait for an answer, since I can see the old bastard is sitting at his desk, probably having gone back to playing solitaire or something.

"Dr. MacDougall, a word?" I ask sharply as I pull Becca inside.

He looks up with disdain. "I thought I might have to endure some theatrics from you, Ms. Magnusson."

My hackles rise, but I don't let him provoke me.

"Can you clarify what Ms. Dillon just told me, please?"

With a theatrical sigh, he folds his arms on the desk in front of him.

"As part of our cutbacks, we've unfortunately had to make the difficult decision to let Ms. Dillon go, effective immediately. If that's unclear, I can use smaller words," he says.

My eyes narrow. The old fucker is *trying* to provoke me. And something smells seriously fishy here.

"I was under the impression that all of the cutbacks had happened the week before last. Nobody else in the hospital was let go today. Why Becca?"

Becca shifts uncomfortably next to me.

"I'm afraid all of that is above your pay grade, so run along and do your job. You wouldn't want to be next, would you?"

I pull my head back and my eyebrows shoot up.

"Was that a *threat?*" I ask sharply.

"Consider it a warning for speaking out of turn," he replies just as harshly. "That kind of insubordination will no longer be tolerated here, and if you don't like it, you'll have to take it up with the Rutherford Group."

"This came from Noah Rutherford?" I clarify.

"As did all the cutbacks, Ms. Magnusson, but that's neither here nor there. Please see yourself out."

I march back to the nurses' station; this time Becca has to race to keep up with me. Sasha looks up in surprise at our abrupt return.

"I take it that didn't go well?" Sasha squeaks.

I shake my head furiously. I look Becca squarely in the eye.

"Go home. I'm going to go have a little talk with Noah Rutherford. Something stinks about all of this, and I'm not taking it lying down. Not this time," I say.

"Jules, please, don't," Becca replies. "I don't want you to put yourself on the line for me. I can find something else. I will find something else. Vincent's already gotten hired on at UCSD Medical. I bet I can too. I'm just … it was just a surprise, that's all. Please, please, please, don't jeopardize your career for me."

I huff. "Oh, Becca, you know me better than that. I already have another job lined up. Don't you worry about me either. But neither of us are going down without a fight."

Sasha looks between us nervously.

"What can I do?" she asks.

"Hold down the fort," I instruct her. "I'll be upstairs."

"Text me later?" Becca asks, looking at us both.

Sasha nods, but I'm too distracted to respond, already formulating what I'm going to say to the bastard in my mind. He hasn't talked to me all week. I thought it was because of how tense things have been between us, but now I'm thinking it might also have been because he was about to do something I didn't like. Since last time he did tell me and that blew up in his face.

He's right about one thing, anyway. He definitely can't win with me.

Becca heads out as I go upstairs. I wring my fingers together anxiously, itching to let it all out.

Once on his floor, I practically race down the hall to his office. The door is open and I enter without knocking. As soon as he looks up, I can tell he knows he's in for it. He rises, going around me to close the door.

He turns, sliding his hands in his pockets, clearly waiting for me to speak first.

I size him up, deciding what I want to say. And I realize I don't want Becca to have to come back to contend with these assholes. And I don't want to keep dealing with this bullshit either.

"Since Dr. MacDougall just made it clear that my particular brand of feedback is no longer welcome here, I'm submitting my resignation to you directly, effective immediately," I say. And fuck if it doesn't feel good. Like a weight is lifted from my chest that I no longer have to play this game of cat and mouse.

Noah's mouth turns down in a frown. "May I ask why?"

"Does it matter?" I snap back, crossing my arms over my chest.

With a sigh, Noah saunters back to his desk chair, sinking into it. "You're an asset to this hospital. I'd like a chance to convince you to stay," he replies.

"Not a chance in hell," I retort. "It was one thing when I thought you were sincerely trying to help, that your hands were tied. But when you turn around and go behind my back to have my friends fired, that's my limit. I'm done. I'm over all these games and all this bullshit. I. Quit." I'm practically giddy with the freedom those words bring. "Have a nice life, Noah."

128

I turn around and leave. I hear him calling after me, but I don't care. About any of it. Not anymore. Stick a fork in me, I'm done.

I head back downstairs.

Sasha looks up once more as I approach.

"I just quit," I inform her.

Her jaw drops and I laugh.

"Are you serious?" she gasps.

"One hundred percent," I assure. "Don't worry, hon. Best decision I ever made."

"But … I …" Sasha stutters, clearly at a loss.

I grab her by the shoulders. "You're going to be just fine, I promise. They'll bring Sarah in for day shift. They'll have to now. She'll help you learn the ropes. And you know we'll see each other plenty. Now, I'm going to get out of here. It'll ruin my dramatic exit if I have to explain myself too much." I give her a wink.

"Well, you seem happy," she finally admits, pulling me into a hug. "Talk later?"

"You bet," I assure her, grabbing my purse. "See you later, my dear."

"Bye, Jules," she says sadly.

But nothing can ruin my high right now. I waltz out of that place with a swagger in my step. I feel like I've finally taken control back. Now I'm going to celebrate with a relaxing bubble bath and some champagne. Hell, I may even wait until next week to start with the private cardiologist's office. Goodness knows I've earned a little break.

Unfortunately, the only break I get is the time it takes me to stop at the grocery store for a celebratory bottle of wine on the drive home. When I get to my place, Noah is sitting on my goddamn front porch. He rises when he sees me approaching.

"Boy, you really don't know when to quit, do you?" I say to him, not even commenting on his complete lack of boundaries in looking up my address.

"Guess I don't," he replies. "But then, seems like you know all about quitting. Care to teach me?" It'd sound playful but for his aggressive demeanor.

"Nope. I'm good. Now, can you please move out of the way? I need to celebrate my new freedom," I snap. He's being a real buzzkill, and I'm already over this conversation.

"First, tell me who was fired," he insists.

I pull a face. "You're not seriously pretending like you don't know," I scoff.

"I'm not in the habit of asking questions to which I already know the answer," he insists testily.

"Are you screwing with me right now?" I ask, seriously confused. "Because Dr. MacDougall explicitly said it was at your direction that Becca was let go."

Noah's jaw tightens. "Then I'll be having a word with Dr. MacDougall, because it *wasn't*."

I look at him skeptically. Dr. MacDougall is a lot of things, but I've never suspected him of lying. Then again, Noah is also a lot of things, but I'm coming to learn he's not the lying type either. The serious-omitter-of-highly-relevant-information type. But liar? No, he's too *principled* for that.

"Whatever, I have to pee, can you please get out of my way?" I demand.

He levels a look at me, but steps aside. I unlock the door and go in, determined to shut the door in his face. But he puts his damn foot on the threshold, stopping me.

"Ugh, whatever, I'll deal with you in a minute," I snap. I really do have to go. One of the worst thing about being a nurse is never getting enough downtime to use the bathroom. It's a long-ago learned habit to hold it until I get home. But any longer and I'm risking a bladder infection. So I just leave the stubborn bastard there and drop the wine bottle on the kitchen counter on my way to the bathroom.

After I've done my business, I kick my shoes off in my room and pull my hair out of its ponytail before heading back to the living room.

Unsurprisingly, Noah is still there, sitting on my damn couch.

"And apparently you can't take a hint either," I remark drily as I head into the kitchen. I grab the bottle of wine and a single wine glass. I bring it back to the living room and sit on the couch next to him, since there's nowhere else to sit, and pour myself a glass of wine.

"What, you're not even going to offer me some?" he asks. And the sourpuss has finally faded into a teasing smirk.

"Nope," I confirm. "I don't offer beverages to uninvited visitors. So what's it going to take to get rid of you?" I take a deep drink of the wine. The liquid is heaven in a glass, and I immediately feel myself relaxing.

"If I promise to talk to Dr. MacDougall about Becca, will you rescind your resignation?" he asks.

"Hmmm, let me think about that," I reply. I take a sip of wine. "Nope." I flash him a grin and take another drink.

"Are you really that happy to get away from me?" he asks, leaning back into the couch.

"God, yes," I admit. "Won't you be glad to not have to worry about pissing me off anymore? Aren't you as exhausted as I am?"

"My main goal is the health of the hospital. My feelings don't matter. And even though I know this has been hard for you, *you're* good for the hospital, Julianna," he persists. "So I'm going to do whatever it takes to get you back."

I drain my glass and set it on the coffee table. I give him a challenging look, but he doesn't comment on my drinking. Smart man.

"First, just talking to him isn't enough. If you can't guarantee that Becca will get her job back, you're wasting my time," I reply.

He raises an eyebrow. "Well, before I can do that, I'm going to need to know why he fired her, so I can't really guarantee anything."

"Except I already told you he said it's because you told him to," I say, exasperated.

"I believe that's what he told you, but management can't always share the real reasons they do things, you know," he insists. "For legal or personal reasons. Who knows. But I can't make any promises without the full story."

"So, you want me to come back on the off chance you *might* unfire her? No thanks."

"What about your job? Your career? Aren't you worried about finding work?" he asks.

"Nope, already have another gig lined up. Any other questions?" I ask with a grin.

That shocks him, and I want to laugh.

"I'll make it worth your while, I promise," he insists.

"I want a ten percent raise," I reply, pouring myself another glass of wine.

"Five," he counters.

"Seven."

"Done."

"I'm still not convinced."

And Noah *laughs*. "This. This is why you have to come back. Who else is going to keep me on my toes?" he asks.

I huff a dry laugh. I should've known. He likes it when we argue. Damn, that explains a lot.

"I'm sure Piper Black is more than capable of keeping you on your toes," I reply drily.

He pulls a face like I'm crazy.

"I'm sorry, were you not photographed on a date with her recently? Did I imagine that picture? Or maybe it was Photoshopped," I say sarcastically.

"Oh, I went out with her," he assures me. "But it was only to take the heat off of you."

"Pffff," I scoff. "Please. I'm not stupid enough to believe that."

"Well, believe it or don't, but please slow down on the wine," he says.

I raise an eyebrow. "Now why on earth would I do that?"

He leans toward me. "Because it's been too damn long since I fucked you, Julianna, and I'd prefer you were completely sober this time."

My whole body clenches at his words. "What makes you think I'm going to hop into bed with you?" I ask shakily. Then, without thinking, I set down my wine glass on the coffee table.

"Who said anything about bed?" he murmurs, his eyes dropping to my lips. It's the only momentary warning I get before he kisses me.

It's different than the first time. Just as hungry, but slower and deeper. Like he's giving me the chance to keep a clear head and stop it if I want.

Part of me wants to stop him. But another part of me remembers what it's like when I don't. I hesitate long enough to where he presses me back on the couch, laying on top of me so that I can feel every inch of his hard body against me. It definitely doesn't help me want to stop.

Still, I break my mouth from his. "We shouldn't," I protest.

He pulls his head back enough so I can look into his eyes.

"We should've, and much sooner," he insists. He leans up, running his hands down my chest. "You have no idea how difficult it's been to resist doing this." He pinches my nipples through my scrubs top and I arch into him. "Or this." His hand drops between my legs, stroking me through the fabric. I can't help the moan that tumbles from my lips.

He takes it as permission, pulling at my bottoms until I'm bared to him. Now his hand wanders, unhindered, to the slickness that's waiting.

"Goddamn," he groans. And without warning, he slips two fingers into me, causing me to gasp and writhe beneath him. There goes any thought of stopping him. Any desire to. "Tell me what you want, Julianna."

"I don't want to think," I reply automatically. "I don't want to be able to think."

With a smirk, he places a thumb on my lips. I suck it hard until he pops it out of my mouth. Then he reaches under my shirt, yanking back my bra cup and swirling his wet thumb around my nipple. I feel it harden under his touch, and the sensation heightens the pleasure he's giving me between my thighs. And it definitely keeps me from thinking about anything but the mind-numbing bliss that I can feel unfurling in my core.

"You're beautiful," he murmurs as he speeds up his assault and pinches my nipple between his thumbs. "Tell me you only come for me."

My breathing hitches. "Only for you."

"Good, baby," he says silkily, pressing his thumb into my clit as he rubs my G-spot inside. "Come now for me, Julianna. I want you to clench that gorgeous pussy of yours around me." As he's speaking, my orgasm floods through me and I do just that. He pumps slower as I unclench, now blissfully blank and happy. Maybe he's right. Maybe we should've been doing this all along. Life is much simpler when you can't think too hard about anything because oxytocin is flooding through your veins.

I close my eyes as his hand stills and withdraws, allowing myself to float in nothingness, my body humming and warm. I hear a zipper being undone. A foil packet being ripped. My body throbs in anticipation.

Strong hands grab my hips, and I open my eyes in time to watch as he flips me onto my stomach, lifting my ass in the air and angling it toward the front of the couch.

"Ohhh, yes," I groan. "Please, give it to me."

"Fuck, Julianna, I could come just from hearing you ask me for it," Noah groans. I feel the tip of his cock pressing at my entrance. He works it up and down, spreading my wetness, teasing me.

"Please, Noah," I beg again.

"Please what?"

I bury my face in the couch and let out a growl of frustration. "Fuck me, dammit. Now," I demand.

His hands clench on my hips, and he buries his cock in me so hard it forces my head into the cushions. Yes. This. This is what I needed. He slams into me mercilessly and my body soars, every nerve ending alight with pleasure.

I'm so steeped in bliss that the only sign of my actual orgasm is the spasming of my walls around Noah's cock. I hear him groan as he finds his own release. When he pulls out, I slump back down to the couch feeling like someone has removed my bones.

I hear Noah walk away. A toilet flushes. A sink runs. Then I hear him return.

"If you keep laying there like that, I'm going to have to do something about it." His deep voice cuts into my cloud of serenity.

I crack an eye open to see him smirking down at me. "Mmm. Like what?" I ask.

He grins and scoops me up with lightning reflexes, carrying me into my bedroom and depositing me carefully on the bed. He kisses me on the mouth, his tongue sweeping against mine briefly before kissing his way down my center, servicing each nipple on his way through the fabric of my top, then moving between my legs. He flattens his tongue against my sex, running it slowly over the whole length of my core a few times before using the tip to tease my clit.

My hips start working without my permission, grinding against his face. Any descent I'd had from my high abruptly vanishes as I'm vaulted back into the clouds, my mind foggy with lust.

I feel Noah's tongue leave me, only to be replaced by the gentle pressure of his finger.

"Tell me you missed this," he demands.

I lift my head to meet his eyes. "I missed you," I admit in a whisper. "Even though you were right there."

"I know exactly how you feel," he assures me, then proceeds to fingerfuck a fourth orgasm out of me before sliding up to mold himself against my jellylike body.

We lay in silence for a while until the fog starts to clear. Though I'm still much less in my head than usual. It's nice. Being with him this way is nice.

"Why couldn't we have more of this and less of being at each other's throats?" I muse out loud. "That would be nice."

"You're the one who didn't call," he reminds me. "I was ready to keep doing this from day one." He gives me a smirk, but I can tell he really means it.

"Yes, well, I think you still like the fighting," I reply.

He laughs, nodding his agreement. "You get all passionate. It's hard not to want to bend you over my desk and fuck you when you're all riled up like that," he responds.

"Yes, well, at least we're well-suited in the bedroom," I reply, finally starting to really come back down to earth. And realizing that we're back to exactly where we started.

"And we're not outside the bedroom?" he asks.

"What does it matter?" I ask rhetorically, rising from the bed. I remove my scrubs top, undershirt, and bra all in one motion so I'm completely naked. "I'm going to take a shower. Want to join me?"

"As tempting as that offer is, I actually need to go back to work," he grumbles. "And don't think for one minute that we're done with this conversation."

"You're not done," I say, "but I am. Enjoy the rest of your day, Noah."

"Does that mean you'll be back to work tomorrow?" he presses, rising from the bed and putting himself in front of me.

"Seven percent raise and you do everything in your power to bring Becca back on?" I ask, pressing my naked body against him. His pupils dilate and his mouth opens. I suppress a triumphant smile.

"That's the deal," he agrees. "Now stop trying to get me to fuck you again."

I let my grin loose. "Oh, Noah," I reply. "If I was trying to get you to fuck me again, you'd know it." I wink and saunter into the bathroom, pleased as punch that my inner confident sex goddess seems to have re-emerged. "Lock the door on your way out."

I turn on the shower and let the steam fill the bathroom. Just as I step into the shower, I hear the front door shut. Jules one, Noah zero. Or actually, Jules four, Noah one. But I'll take it anyway.

# CHAPTER 15

I go back to work the next morning, much to Sasha's surprise. I promise to tell her later, when we're not at work. I definitely don't want to restart the rumors about Noah and me.

Becca is likewise back at work by lunchtime. She doesn't say a word, simply high-fiving me on the way in. That's Becca.

MacDougall is furious. We normally don't see much of him, but he spends the day hovering and huffing and asking all kinds of nosy questions.

Part of me is smug at my victory. The other part of me wonders what the hell he's up to and if I'm going to regret my power play.

Early that afternoon I get paged to the nurses' station while I'm cleaning up after a procedure. When I get back to the desk, Becca hands me my cellphone.

"It's been buzzing constantly," she says. "The number isn't in your phone book, but I didn't want to turn it off in case it was an emergency."

"Thanks," I reply, going to put it in my pocket, but before I can manage to, it buzzes again.

"Hello?" I answer.

"Hey, beautiful," Noah's voice says over the line.

"Are you seriously calling me while I'm at work?" I ask with a laugh.

"I'm seriously calling you while you're at work. I didn't want to wait too long to ask you to go to dinner with me tomorrow night."

"Can't. We always do team happy hour Friday evenings." Which I may or may not actually attend, but I don't tell him that. Best to keep him on his toes. Especially since he apparently likes that.

"Hmm. Saturday then?"

I hesitate, knowing going on a real date with him is an awful idea. But the guy did just get my friend unfired and secured me a huge raise.

"Fine."

"I'll pick you up at seven," he replies, and I can hear the smile in his voice. I hate myself for it, but it makes me smile too.

"I'll see you then," I agree.

"Not if I see you first," he teases.

I roll my eyes and hang up, handing it back to Becca. "You can put it back in the locker," I tell her.

She looks at me expectantly. "Well?"

"Not here," I say in a low voice. But I give her a wink. "Tell you later."

She waggles her eyebrows and grins. "I'ma hold you to that, boo."

I round the corner to go back to the exam room and finish up, but I run smack into MacDougall.

"Ms. Magnusson, please come with me," he says curtly.

I look at him in bewilderment. "Why?"

And by the irritation on his face, I half expect him to bellow "Insubordination!" then and there. Thankfully, he doesn't. He simply turns and stalks away, pretending I didn't ask. So I follow. Sure that nothing good will come of it, but also sure I don't really have much of a choice.

He heads into his office, seating himself in his chair and gesturing for me to sit. I perch on the edge, bracing myself.

He opens a drawer and grabs what appears to be some sort of form. He spends a few minutes filling it in while I sit in confused silence. Finally, he turns it toward me and slides it across the desk with a pen.

"This is a conduct warning that will be added to your file. Please read it and sign at the bottom," he directs haughtily.

I suppress an eye roll and look down at the form, scanning the few lines he'd filled in under my name, employee number, and the date and time.

"I'm being written up for personal use of a cellphone while at work?" I ask, aghast. "Are you kidding me?"

"I'm not 'kidding you,' Ms. Magnusson. I witnessed it myself. Sign the form."

"I want to see the rule that says I'm not allowed to do that," I insist. "Because I've never heard of it."

"Really?" he scoffs. "Because there are signs all over the hospital, Ms. Magnusson. Let's not play these games."

The irony. Oh, the irony.

"Those signs *request* that *patients* not use their cellphones while in the hospital. They do not *forbid* the *employees* from using them," I point out. "We all put our cellphones in a locker to minimize the potential for equipment interference. But emergencies happen, so sometimes we need to answer our phones."

I realize I'm wasting my breath, but I can't not fight this totally bogus write-up.

"Yes, well, I might be willing to overlook such a case, but your call was *clearly* personal in nature," he replies with a sniff.

"I had no control over the nature of the call, and I kept it brief. Are you seriously writing me up for this? Because I'm not an idiot. I know that repeated warnings can give you grounds on which to fire me."

He looks startled for a moment before he composes himself, and I know I just hit the nail on the head. He's been hanging around looking for reasons to write me up so he could fire me. Or maybe Becca. More likely both of us, in punishment for going around him. I should've known.

"Then perhaps you shouldn't have violated the policies *you* signed when you started working here," he responds.

That makes me laugh out loud. I can't help it. "You realize when I started working here I was eighteen years old? Do you remember if we had a cellphone policy on the books in 2003? Because I sure as hell don't. I want to see where I signed agreeing to that before I'll sign this write-up," I insist.

"You'll sign this right now or you'll be written up for noncompliance as well," he replies, going purple in the face. "And with two on the books, I'll be well within my rights to submit your termination paperwork."

I raise my eyebrows. "And I'm well within my rights to request that we involve administration at this point, as I feel I'm being threatened into signing something I don't think is valid," I respond. I rise from the chair. "Shall we?"

MacDougall sits there, sputtering for a bit before he purses his lips. "I don't think that will be necessary."

"Oh, I think it is," I insist, snatching the paper from the desktop before he can retrieve and destroy it. "I can go on my own, if you prefer not to join me."

"I … that is to say …" he stammers. "I'm too busy for that sort of thing at the moment. Get back to work." He turns purposefully toward his computer, ignoring me with all of his might.

I take the write-up with me, chuckling on my way back to the nurses' station. Becca looks up curiously at my amusement.

"What?" she asks.

I jerk my head toward the door. "Take a walk with me and I'll tell you."

She raises an eyebrow but joins me. As soon as we're off the unit, I tell her what happened and warn her that he clearly has it out for me, and probably her too.

"Damn, so are we headed to administration next?" she asks.

I wave a hand, folding the piece of paper into my breast pocket. "Of course not. Not unless he forces my hand, anyway. But I will document this in an email and send it to myself. Just in case. But I wanted to warn you first so you didn't fall into any of his traps."

Becca blows out a breath. "Geez, well, this is going to be fun," she says sarcastically as we make our way back to cardiac.

I pat her on the back as we get to the desk. "Don't worry, it won't last forever. I have a plan."

"Oooh, I like the sound of this," she replies gleefully. "What can I do to help?"

I give her a wink. "Just be you, babe. Just be you. And let me know if anything happens, okay?"

She gives me a salute. "You got it, boss." She looks at me funny for a second. "You know, you seem different."

"I feel different," I admit. "I think having a fallback plan, being able to quit if I want to, gave me a new perspective. It's liberating."

"Well, whatever put that smile on your face, I'm all for it," she responds. "For a second I thought you might be gettin' some. But ya know, the whole liberated woman thing is cool too."

That gets a laugh out of me. "Can I tell you a secret, Becks?" She leans in with an eager look, and I drop my voice so even if you were standing ten feet away you wouldn't be able to hear. "It might be a little of both."

Becca's eyes go wide and she doesn't respond out loud, simply holding up a hand for a high five and doing a little dance on the spot. With a chuckle, I high-five her, then we both go about our business.

When I have a lull later that afternoon, I go see a couple of old friends in different parts of the hospital.

I hit up Ben Ferris in billing first, having known him almost the whole time I've been at Rutherford. I even introduced him to his now-wife. So when I ask him to compare MacDougall's appointment charts with insurance claims and patient invoices for the last year, he doesn't bat an eyelash, and I know he'll keep his mouth shut.

Same for Tara Scopes in what's basically the human resources area of hospital administration; we've been good friends for more than a decade, and she happily agrees to quietly research MacDougall's history of employee write-ups.

I leave work at the end of the day finally feeling like I'm regaining some modicum of control over the chaos that has become my life. And hoping like hell it's not all about to blow up in my face.

# CHAPTER 16

I'm sifting through patient files on Friday afternoon when Sasha approaches the nurses' station with an air of urgency that immediately puts me on high alert.

"I was just called into MacDougall's office," she hisses to Becca and me before we can say a word. "They're moving me to the cardiovascular intensive care unit."

"What the hell?" Becca asks angrily, but I hold up a hand.

"And they're moving Sarah to day shift here, yes?" I ask Sasha.

She looks at me, bewildered. "Yes, how'd you know that?"

I shake my head, not wanting to get into it here. "Later. They're promoting you to ARNP though, right?"

Sasha nods. "And supposedly giving me a raise, but the ICU chief will go over all that with me on Monday," she agrees.

"Wait … so what's the problem with this?" Becca asks, confused.

"I … guess there's not one? I was just worried it would upset you guys," Sasha admits.

"Well, I mean, it'll suck not getting to talk as much as we normally do, but you'll just be right down the hall,"

Becca replies with a shrug. "And you know, more money for you, so yay."

"You don't look very 'yay,'" I point out drily. "But I have to get into exam eleven, so you can tell me why at happy hour."

"Aw, hell yes, you're coming?" Becca asks, looking significantly more chipper.

I chuckle. "Wouldn't miss it," I reply with a wink. "See you ladies there?"

"See you there," they say in unison.

\* \* \*

It's nearly seven by the time I make it to our usual happy hour spot a few blocks from the hospital, and as soon as I'm inside I can hear the lot of them loudly chatting and laughing from the booth they occupy across the room. And seeing as the place is pretty packed, that's saying something.

I make my way over, hoping that means everyone is starting to feel better about their lives and their jobs, after everything that's been going down.

As I approach, I note that it's more or less the usual crowd: Sasha and Cal on one side, Becca and Mark at the back, and Zoe and Ethan opposite Sasha and Cal. It's almost like three happy couples, except Zoe and Ethan are just friends, and Mark only wishes he were with Becca. Hopefully, now that Vincent's working across town and not able to join happy hour anymore, that won't give Mark any ideas. Not that Becca can't take care of herself.

In any case, they all greet me as I approach, and Sasha slides over to let me sit next to her. I give her a squeeze around the shoulder and congratulate her on her promotion, realizing I hadn't done that earlier.

# YOU CAN'T BUY LOVE

We talk a bit about the switch, then as soon as I'm sure nobody else is paying attention, I give her the highlights of my conversation with Noah about shuffling her and Sarah, apologizing for not mentioning it sooner. It's hard to remember what I have and haven't told people these days. The drama has been very real and pretty overwhelming.

Thankfully, Sasha's not one to hold grudges or pay much attention to what other people say or do anyway. And I know not working with Cal will take some of the pressure off keeping their relationship under wraps. So it all worked out in the end.

I don't miss the looks Ethan shoots me through a couple of rounds of drinks. Unfortunately, after my second beer, I get up to use the ladies room only to find that Zoe has gone home to her wife, leaving Ethan's side of the booth conspicuously empty. As much as I'd like to avoid his advances, I'd also rather not make it look like I'm scared of him by insisting on sitting next to Sasha anyway.

So I resignedly slide into the booth next to him, giving him a small, forced smile.

"So, what'd I miss?" I ask, trying to engage the whole table so as to avoid solo talk with Ethan.

"You'll never guess who came in while you were gone," Mark says with quiet excitement, pointing at the bar.

I turn, already suspecting who I'm going to see. Yep. Noah. Accepting a beer from the bartender. Thankfully, his back is to us and he's across the room. I turn back, wishing the sight away. What the hell is he doing here?

"What the hell is he doing here?" Becca whispers angrily, voicing my thought verbatim.

I shrug, trying to play it off. "Obviously, the same thing we are," I reply. "It *is* the closest bar to the hospital, after all."

Sasha gives me an *Are you okay?* look that I choose to ignore.

"Dude, we should invite him over," Mark says obliviously. "Maybe he'll buy us all beers. That's what rich guys do, right?"

I arch an eyebrow. "You obviously don't know Noah Rutherford," I grumble.

And like he heard, Noah turns and our eyes meet across the room.

I'm spellbound, staring at him, not daring to breathe. Hoping nobody notices that I can't take my eyes off him.

But I needn't worry, as in mere moments he looks away. Like he barely recognized me. Like he doesn't know or care about me.

I should be happy about that, but I find myself annoyed anyway. That he's here. That he's for some reason acting like I don't matter. I don't even care if it's to spare me having to explain what's going on between us to my friends. For some reason, I just can't shake the slight.

"You okay, Jules?" Ethan asks quietly from next to me, putting his hand on my thigh.

I look down at the hand and then back up at him. My, he's bold today. I reach down and give his hand a squeeze, subtly moving it to the seat between us.

"Great, thanks," I assure him. "How are you doing, Ethan?"

He grins widely at the perceived encouragement. "Much better now you're back," he says. I sigh internally.

Unfortunately, everyone else at the table has moved to individual conversations too, and I'm forced to make small talk with Ethan for a while. He keeps touching me in little ways — mostly on my hand, arm, and shoulder — and looking dreamily into my eyes.

I wish I wanted someone like Ethan. Someone who was sweet, steady, and eager to please. He's everything Noah isn't. Yet somehow, here I am, bored to tears and unable to stop thinking about Noah Rutherford.

Thankfully, once our glasses start running low again, and it's so busy our waitress hasn't been by in a while, the guys decide to go get us another round, leaving Sasha, Becca, and I at the table together.

"I think I'm going to bail before the guys get back," I say, faking a yawn. "Becca, I trust you can handle the extra beer?"

She cracks a smirk. "Oh, I sure can, but let's call a spade a spade here. Which one are you running from: Noah or Ethan?"

I shake my head and huff a dry laugh. "I don't know, both?"

Becca looks over my shoulder. "Whelp, you didn't run fast enough," she mutters.

I turn my head in time to find Noah closing in, looking grim-faced.

"Ladies," he greets us curtly. "Ms. Magnusson, may I have a word?"

Before I can even respond, he grasps me firmly by the elbow and steers me out of the booth. I only have time to give a bewildered look and gesture of *WTF* toward Sasha and Becca before he's pulled me through the crowd to the hall that leads to the restrooms.

He pulls me past both the men's and women's rooms, to the gender-neutral stall at the very back. It's only once he's pulled me inside and closed and locked the door behind him that it's quiet enough to protest.

"What the hell, Noah?" I growl up at him.

He grabs me by the shoulders in answer, turning me away from him and planting my hands on the flower-papered wall. He presses himself behind me, his fingers finding their way to my breasts, his breath hot on my ear. No kissing. No caressing. Only raw need that borders on anger.

"Don't talk," he commands.

I open my mouth to protest when one of his hands drops down the front of my pants, roughly grabbing my sex, stroking between my lower lips. My back arches and no words of dissent escape me, only a throaty moan. It's so sudden, but it feels so damn good.

"I'm going to fuck you right here, baby," he promises gruffly in my ear, both of his hands dropping to my waistband and sharply tugging my scrubs bottoms to my ankles. An instant later I hear a zipper, then the rip of foil, then his hard cock on my backside. I hate it, but I'm so turned on, already soaking wet and wanting him inside me.

So when he sinks deep into me, I greedily tilt to accept him, using the leverage of my arms on the wall to get him all the way in.

His hands grasp my hips an instant before he starts a punishing rhythm. My core tightens around every hard thrust, the pleasure ripping through me. But in mere minutes, I feel him pick up speed, hear his breath hitch, then feel him pulsate inside me as he groans out his orgasm. He gives one final, mighty thrust, burying himself completely in me. His front joins to my back, his arms encircling me so we're fully connected.

"You're mine, Julianna," he utters in my ear. "Nobody else's. Do you hear me?"

"I'm not a possession," I say, panting. I shuffle to work his cock out of me, and he grabs the condom to stop his cum from spilling all over.

I turn to face him, putting my back against the wall.

"Is that what this is about? Marking your territory?" I ask angrily.

"I saw that guy you were sitting with. He doesn't get to touch you like that anymore," Noah says, tying off the condom, tossing it in the trash, and pulling up his pants.

I make to pull mine up, but he stops me.

"And you don't get to tell me what to do," I snap.

"I'm not done yet," he growls, dropping into a squat, his tongue finding its way between my legs. His fingers follow, sinking deep into me while he laps at the wetness he made between my thighs.

"Fuck," I gasp, grabbing him hard by the hair. My first thought was to pull him away from me, to rail at him that he doesn't get to tell me who I spend time with, who touches me, but I find myself angrily pressing him into me harder, opening my knees, relishing in the pleasure he's giving me.

His wicked tongue scrapes across my clit as his fingers pump furiously over the spot inside. An orgasm builds so fast and furiously that I don't have time to think about how fucked up this is before I'm choking back screams from my orgasm.

He pulls away and I slump back, catching my breath as he wipes his face and washes his hands.

Once I'm collected enough, I stand up and fix my clothes, then turn to him.

"I can't do this, Noah," I spit at him as he throws the paper towel in the garbage can and faces me. "One minute you're on my side, saying all the right things, acting like a good guy. The next you're an arrogant, entitled, possessive asshole. This isn't going to work. I can't date you."

"Oh, really? Your mood swings seem plenty capable of keeping up with me," he retorts.

My hands fly to my hips. "Fine, we're both all over the goddamn map with each other," I allow. "But that's my point. This isn't me. This isn't what I want."

Someone bangs on the door.

"Occupied," Noah snarls loudly. Then he turns back to me. "Then let's get off this damn rollercoaster. Together."

I shake my head. Why does this all have to be so complicated? "I'm not the one who tried to fuck you into submission. Goodbye, Noah."

I let myself out to run smack into a very confused-looking guy who clearly was waiting for the larger, private bathroom. I can't even imagine what the look will be on his face when Noah comes out next, and I don't care. I walk straight out of the damn bar without looking back.

# CHAPTER 17

"I can't handle this anymore, Becks," I groan first thing Monday morning. "If I have to keep working in the same hospital as that man, I'm going to lose my shit."

Becca rolls her eyes. "Girl, I've got the market cornered on overly dramatic, and you're putting even me to shame. Chillax. I mean, seriously, you don't even have to see him almost ever, and I'm sure all this shit will be done at some point."

I shake my head. "He's like a disturbance in the force," I insist. "Even when he's not right here, he's messing with my life. Like that whole rumor about us."

"Please," Becca scoffs. "Nobody's even talking about that anymore. And they wouldn't have been talking about it in the first place if you guys weren't stupid enough to go up to his hotel room *together*. Note for next time, boo: He goes first, then you meet him there, nobody's the wiser."

I pull a confused face. "I'm sorry, do you know something I don't?" I ask. "Did someone see us?"

"Ohhhh, fuuuuuuck," Becca says, her eyes going wide. "I forgot to tell you, didn't I?"

I snap my head back. "Oh my god, yes, you did," I exclaim. She looks at me sheepishly. "Well? Spill it already!"

"All right, all right, yeesh," she replies theatrically. "The rumor mill may have passed down that the chief of emergency saw you two leaving the gala together. Hand in hand. And getting into an elevator to the bank of rooms over the ballroom area."

"And they went spreading that around? Holy fucking shit," I gasp.

"Ehhhh, I think it was more like they told one person, in confidence, who obviously couldn't keep their mouth shut," she allows, with the clear air of understanding as someone who has done exactly that more than once. "Either way, sounds like you guys weren't exactly discreet about it. And at least it wasn't Moneybags himself who couldn't keep his mouth shut."

"Oh, because that gets him off the hook for being a domineering bastard," I grumble.

"Jules. Darling. The price you pay for a man who gets you all worked up in bed is that sometimes he's gonna get you all worked up other places, and not always in a good way," she says patiently. "It just goes with the whole dynamic."

"Well, then you and Vincent must have off-the-charts amazing sex because you guys sure do bitch at each other in public enough," I tease.

She bobs her head on her neck. "You know it. And really. You must know it, because you and this guy are obviously at each other's throats. And I'm still waiting to hear how *hot* that must mean things are between the sheets." She purses her lips and looks at me expectantly.

I heave a deep sigh. "It's like my birthday and Christmas and a Marvin Gaye song all wrapped up in one," I admit. "But that's not the point."

"Oh, I think that's *exactly* the point, darling," she replies, with laughter in her voice. "But I see you've got a ways to go before you realize that. It's all good. Take your time."

We're interrupted by Ben Ferris appearing around the corner with a sheaf of papers nestled in the crook of one arm.

"Ah, Jules," he greets me with a smile. "I have something I think you're going to like."

I hop out of my chair, gesturing for him to come around the corner.

"We have fifteen minutes until our morning meeting, so I'm all ears," I assure him.

Ben plunks the stack onto the desktop, pulling the top sheet off the pile.

"This is the summary report," he points at the rest, "and that is the backup." He points to a bold number at the bottom of the left column. "Bottom line? That's the total amount that should have been billed for all of our subject's patients in the last year between both patient responsibility and what insurance would actually cover." He points to a number in the right column just to the side of the first number that's almost three times as much. "That's how much was collected from both the patients and insurance combined."

My eyes grow wide and my heart leaps in my chest. "Were the patients overcharged or was the insurance overbilled?" I ask tersely.

"Both," he replies. "Including insurance billing charges for procedures there is no record of being performed."

I gasp. No. Fucking. Way. Holier-than-thou MacDougall has been committing billing and insurance fraud.

"Yes, big deal," he murmurs. He fishes a thumb drive from his pocket. "It's all on here too, and I've got it saved to one of my own. I'm required to report these findings, but if you had a plan to do so first, I can wait a day at most."

I look up at him and let out a sigh of relief. "I have one more thing to follow up on, then I'll take this straight to Noah Rutherford this morning," I assure him. "Thank you, Ben, I really owe you."

He smiles. "Honestly, you've done me a favor. I'll get major kudos for bringing this issue to light," he replies. "But you're welcome. And Trish says hi, by the way."

"Tell her hi back," I reply with a distracted smile, grabbing the sheaf of papers. With a wave, Ben disappears back down the hall, and I turn to Becca.

"Don't worry about the staff meeting, I'll cover for you," she assures me, clearly having paid attention to every word. "Go get it done, boo."

Suddenly, I'm giddy, and I can't help but unleash a grin. "I'm going to go see Tara before heading up to Noah's office."

Becca nods and salutes. "See you when I see you."

I nod, too preoccupied for much else, and head up to Noah's floor, since Tara's office is at the other end of his hall.

Unfortunately, when I get there, she doesn't have anything else incriminating. He's pretty much written up everyone at some point or another. Guess I shouldn't be that surprised. But I don't need anything more from her anyway. Not with what I got from Ben.

So I march straight to Noah's office. I knock with my free hand but don't get an answer. So I knock again, impatient to share this information with him. When I still get no response, I try the handle, and it pops right open.

Noah looks up at me from his desk, aghast, and clearly on a phone call.

"It's important," I mouth.

His nostrils flare and his eyes tighten, but he wraps up the call and gestures for me to enter.

"It damn well better be *very* important for you to interrupt me like that," he says in a threatening tone.

I drop the stack of papers on his desk, passing him the summary report. "Oh, I think you're going to want to look at this report as soon as possible," I assure him smugly. I let his eyes scan the paper for a minute. When his jaw drops, I know he's understood. "See, Dr. MacDougall made it very clear to me last week that he was going to do everything in his power to have me fired after deducing that I had something to do with getting Becca back. So rather than wait, I asked a couple of key people to help me look into his goings-on at the hospital a little further, concerned that he'd tried to pull something similarly shady in the past. But even I never dreamed he'd be involved in something this big."

Noah's eyes snap up to meet mine. "Do you mean to say others are involved?" he asks sharply.

I realize my phrasing did imply that. "No, I just meant that I didn't imagine him doing this sort of thing," I clarify.

"Nonetheless, that he could even get away with something like this merits further investigation as to how long it has been going on and how it's been overlooked," he says in a stern tone. Then he drops the paper on his desk and sinks back into his chair, rubbing his eyes. "Thank you for bringing it to my attention."

I stand there for a moment, trying not to feel like his reaction was slightly anticlimactic, or be annoyed by his curt dismissal, but after a minute I head for the door. Just before I leave, I decide to ask the question that's been bugging me all weekend.

"Noah?" He looks up. "Did you know I'd be at that bar on Friday?"

He drops his hands in his lap, looking completely worn out.

"No, Julianna. I didn't know you'd be at that bar on Friday."

His words sound truthful, but I hold his gaze for a moment longer, looking for any sign of deception. But I find none. It would be so much easier if I did. With a small nod, I turn and leave.

* * *

The week crawls by with a heavy sense of anticipation. But nothing happens. Nor for the week after. Every day that ticks by has me looking over my shoulder, wondering if MacDougall somehow was confronted, wormed his way out of trouble, and is about to rain hell down on me. So many times I almost go to Noah's office to ask. But I'm finally learning to ignore the fact that he's working in an office only a few floors over my head. So I let it be.

But two weeks to the day after I brought Noah the evidence on MacDougall, I arrive at my usual five-thirty in the morning start time to Dr. Carson waiting with Sarah at the nurses' station. And they're both just standing there. Dr. Carson looks grim, Sarah looks nervous.

"Morning, guys," I say hesitantly. "Any reason you're looking like doom and gloom this morning?"

"Jules," Dr. Carson greets me. "Now that you're here, let's all go have a chat in my office."

He ruffles a hand through his gray head of hair as he leads us down the hall and around the corner. But he doesn't turn into the last office on the left like I expect. No, he hooks a right into MacDougall's office. An office that, as I enter, I realize has been stripped bare but for the furniture.

"No," I gasp in disbelief. Even though I'd expected MacDougall would be fired. Hell, I'd *hoped* for it.

Dr. Carson settles himself in the chair behind the large, dark wood desk.

"I'm afraid so," he confirms.

Sarah and I sink into the chairs across from him.

"What happened?" Sarah asks, confused.

Dr. Carson gives me a loaded look. "Where to begin?" he muses. After a moment of thought, he resumes. "It will be announced this morning that four hospital officials have been replaced, and each job role in each unit has been given a new title and salary assignment to align with the new hospital budgets and staffing goals. It was always part of the overall reorganization plan to ask Dr. MacDougall to retire, but unfortunately evidence was brought to light that, upon deeper investigation, outed him, two other chiefs, and Mrs. Knowles as having collaborated to commit financial fraud against both our patients and the insurance companies. That last part is information not to be shared outside of this room."

We both gasp and nod. Not in my wildest dreams did I think this went as high as Mrs. Knowles.

"So you're our new chief," I deduce.

"That I am, Jules," he responds. "Though I suppose I could start calling you 'Ms. Magnusson' now." He gives me a wink to show he's joking.

I snort. "Jules is fine," I assure him drily.

"You said something about budgets and staffing goals?" Sarah points out.

"Ah, yes, that," he responds. "All of the chiefs, including the newly appointed ones, have been consulted over these last six weeks on patient volume, projected growth, and required staffing. After cutting what the Rutherford Group deemed to be individuals unfit to represent our organization, hiring to that staffing plan has been fully funded under new procedures to ensure candidates are both hired in a controlled and fair manner consistent with local, state, and federal regulations, as well as meet the job qualifications without bias."

Sarah and I share a meaningful look. Translation: no more hiring friends and friends of friends. No more hiring people just to get warm bodies in here. *Halle-freaking-lujah.*

"What about raises?" I press.

Dr. Carson smiles, obviously pleased with what he's about to share. "Oh, you're going to like this part," he responds. "Based on the newly defined job roles and target salaries, all hospital personnel's salaries will be adjusted accordingly — only upward, mind you — to put them at the appropriate salary based on their performances for those years they would've gotten raises. Plus, there will be an extra boost if needed to put everyone's compensation on par with industry standards. In some cases we're not talking about a lot of money, but it will counteract much of the disparity in pay across functions and encourage those who are still here to stay onboard long term. At least, I think that's the hope."

"Well, it sure won't hurt," Sarah snarks. She's always been particularly bitter, not having been granted the overnight shift pay differential the hospital offered back when she started. Not that she'll get that anyway, but it sounds like we'll all receive sizeable raises.

I wonder briefly if I'll get less since I already negotiated a pretty hefty hike out of Noah. And as soon as I remember him, a thought pops into my mind.

"Who will replace Mrs. Knowles?" I ask abruptly.

"For the time being, Noah Rutherford," Dr. Carson responds, confirming my suspicion. "But I believe the long-term plan is to identify candidates from within Rutherford Hospital or one of the other hospitals in the Rutherford Group family to fill that role."

"I see," I respond softly, looking down into my hands. I can feel tears pricking the backs of my eyes, and I blink them away, unsure of why I'm so emotional. Then again, all these changes are huge. Maybe being emotional about it isn't such a strange reaction.

"Any other questions?" Dr. Carson prompts.

"Not at the moment," Sarah responds carefully.

I shake my head.

"All right then, ladies. Let's go get this show on the road," he replies, rising.

I take a deep breath and follow. Glad for once to have news that's going to make things better.

# CHAPTER 18

The mood throughout the hospital borders on party-like the whole week. I've seriously never seen everyone this happy to work here, this excited about changes being made. It's the feeling I've been trying to get back for *years*, and I want to cry with happiness.

On Thursday, however, I'm jolted back to reality when Lisa passes along that Noah wants to see me in his office at the end of my shift. Instead of worrying about butting heads with him, I purposefully decide to take it as an opportunity to thank him. It's the least I can do as, in the end, he really did deliver.

But it's also hard not to be nervous about why he wants to see me. Still, I power through, and work is still busy enough to keep me from thinking too hard about anything else

The end of my shift is upon me before I know it, and I stand once again at Noah's office door. You think I'd be used to it by now. With a snort at my own inner snark, I lift my hand and knock.

The familiar call of, "Come in," follows. I take a deep breath and open the door to the usual scene. Noah, handsome as ever, busy at his desk in a fitted gray dress shirt rolled to the elbows and black slacks. And when his honeyed eyes meet mine, it's every bit as jarring as it always is.

"You wanted to see me?" I ask, standing behind one of the chairs in front of his desk.

He looks at me, then looks at the chair, then looks back at me. But he wisely doesn't say a word. I suppress a smile at his lack of ordering me to sit down for once.

"I wanted to tell you I was able to match your mother with a program that will cover almost all of her care," he explains, picking up a few pieces of paper and handing them to me. "Since you have health care power of attorney, you'll need to be the one to authorize it. Just call the number circled there and reference the program listed beneath it."

I take the papers, absolutely stunned.

"I ... wow, Noah ..." I look down at the sheet, and sure enough the details listed seem to match my mother's situation. It also says the program is invitation only, so clearly I have Noah's influence to thank for this opportunity. In any case, between this program and the Alzheimer's drug trial my dad is in, I'll be paying less than a quarter of what I'd previously paid out of pocket.

And that's when it hits me. I look back up at him sharply. "You got my dad into that Alzheimer's trial too, didn't you?"

Noah freezes, and I know it's true.

"Yes," he admits. "I did." He looks at me, clearly wary of what's about to come.

"Why?" I demand.

He looks at me with ... pity? No, that's not it. Something else I can't quite place.

"Can't you just be happy that I helped? Does it matter why?" he asks.

"Oh, now I really want to know," I insist. "What are you hiding, Noah?"

He takes a deep breath and stands to close the door. Seems like we have a lot of closed-door conversations. Ones that usually leave me pissed off. I brace myself for whatever he's about to say when he turns back to me.

He stands, not a half dozen feet away, staring at me with a vulnerability that's heartrending.

"Because I love you, Julianna," he admits. "And I'm doing everything I know how to make you mine."

I'm shocked into silence. No, "shocked" is an understatement. There are no words for what I feel right now.

My throat constricts.

War erupts inside me.

He's lying. He can't love me, I've been such a jerk to him. He's light years out of my league. I'm not the kind of woman someone like him would be with. So … why would he lie? Is he trying to manipulate me? To god only knows what end. Knowing how deluded with power and out of touch with reality people like him are, it's not out of the question.

Or worse, he's telling the truth. Maybe he thinks he loves me, but it's just because I've refused him? He's certainly a man who isn't used to being told no. The thrill of the chase and all. Forbidden fruit. Yes, that's it. This is another power trip. And he thinks he can get what he wants by buying me off. And once he's gotten it, he'll cast me aside when it's no longer fun.

I clench my fists at my sides, knowing I just can't take the chance either way. I've been hurt by men with far less power over me than him. Love is a gamble that rarely pays

164

off under the best of circumstances. And I can't afford the risk.

"You can't buy love, Noah," I finally say, my voice thick with emotion. "Especially not mine."

"I haven't bought anything," he insists, frustration clear in his tone.

I open my eyes and laugh.

"Yes, you have," I respond. "You've bartered your influence, your name, to get things other people can't. And while I appreciate what you've done for my parents, the fact that your privilege got those things won't make me love you. Though I'll forever be in your debt."

I swallow hard and shake my head. The idea of being indebted to someone like him is hard to stomach. But even I'm not so stubborn as to look a gift horse in the mouth. Knowing my parents will be cared for in their last, difficult years, no matter what happens to me, isn't something I can walk away from.

"I should go," I murmur. "Thank you." I lift the papers. "For this. And for everything else. For what it's worth, you've earned my trust." Limited to anything but my heart, though it may be. But I don't say that part.

Noah steps forward, dangerously close, looking down at me. "But not your respect," he deduces.

I can't look him in the eye. Because there's a war raging inside me.

"It's hard to respect someone who won't leave you to make your own choices without trying to influence them," I explain. "I need space, Noah."

"I'm afraid to give it to you," he admits, his eyes glistening. He looks away and sniffs deeply, but when he looks back at me, he's fully composed. "Besides, you're stuck with me until we find a new hospital director, I'm afraid."

A tightness spreads through my chest at that thought. At the idea that he may pop up at any moment, pressuring me with his affections, his expectations. I weigh that against the thought of leaving. And I know which hurts less right now.

"Then I think it may be time for me to move on," I reply, sadness lacing my voice. "You have things well in hand here. I trust it'll all be fine without me now."

Noah's features tighten, and he studies my face for what feels like an age.

"Don't quit just yet. Give me a day. Let me see what I can do."

My brows pull together in confusion. "I'm not sure what good that will do. But okay, fine. One day."

Noah steps backward and turns to the door, holding it open for me.

"Thank you again," I say awkwardly. "For … everything."

"It was my pleasure," he replies with a small smile.

I nod but don't say anything else, simply walking out. Though really, there's nothing simple about it.

\* \* \*

I wake up in that black part of night that feels timeless, panting and sweating. The dream that woke me still fully vivid in my mind. Well, memory, I should say.

*Sheila's mom pulls up at the curb to my house, and I can't get out of the car fast enough.*

*"It'll be okay, Jules, you'll see," Sheila calls after me. "I'm sure something else happened at the dance after we*

166

*left, and by Monday nobody will remember anything Heather and her stupid friends said."*

*I wave dismissively, not even bothering with a response as I stomp up the walkway into the house.*

*The front door flies open under my angry shove, and my mother comes running out of the kitchen, drying her hands on a dish towel.*

*"Heavens, Julianna, you scared me," she chides. "What's going on?"*

*Her eyes run over my angry face, clenched fists, and disheveled tulle nightmare of a dress. Just hours ago I was fawning over it. Now, it's a mess from being angrily picked at on the car ride home.*

*"Bobby Cordero asked me to dance," I snap.*

*She raises an eyebrow. "And that's a bad thing? Am I missing something?" she asks, throwing the towel she's holding over her shoulder. "I thought you had a crush on him."*

*I fold my arms across my chest. "Crushes are for little girls, Mom," I scoff.*

*She tries to hide her amused smile, but it just makes me angrier. Or maybe it's because she just stands there, waiting for an explanation. Or maybe it's because I do like him.*

*I sigh heavily and roll my eyes. "He only asked me because Heather Adams wouldn't dance with him," I explain.*

*"So? What does that matter? Didn't you want to dance with him?" she asks.*

*This time my hands go to my hips. "I don't want to be his second choice. That's embarrassing, Mom," I sass back.*

*"How do you even know that's why he wanted to dance with you? Surely he didn't say that?" she asks pointedly.*

*"Because I did dance with him," I say, tears of humiliation running down my face. "Then Heather told me after that he only danced with me because she said no."*

*"Ah, I see. So what happened then?"*

*I bite my lip and shake my head, tears continuing to spill down my face. My mom steps forward and wraps her arms around me.*

*"Come on, baby girl," she says gently. "You can tell me. Let it out."*

*I push against her, angrier still at being called a baby.*

*"If you must know," I snap, "he was standing right there, and he didn't say* anything. *He just turned all red and left. Then Heather and all her friends started laughing at me. It was so embarrassing, Mom."*

*She looks at me with sympathy written all over her face. "That does sound pretty awful. I'm so sorry, Julianna. Why don't you go get changed and I'll make you some cocoa?"*

*I sniff deeply, considering rejecting her offer, just to dish out some of the rejection I'm feeling. But cocoa sounds too good to resist. So I nod and go clean up.*

*Not long later, I'm sitting at the kitchen table in my PJs sipping the warm, sweet drink gratefully when my mom slides into the chair next to me with her own mug. She places a hand on my arm.*

*"I know you probably don't want to hear this right now, but as awful as Heather was, and as cowardly as it was for Bobby to leave, that doesn't mean she was right. Maybe he did want to dance with you. And maybe he only left because he was embarrassed by her too."*

*I look up and give her the stink eye.*

"Doesn't matter," I grumble. "I'm still going to be a laughingstock at school on Monday."

"Oh, I think it does matter," she argues. "Maybe if you give Bobby a chance to explain you two can band together to show everyone Heather was wrong and just being a bully."

"But what if she was right?" I point out. "I'd rather just keep my head down and let it all blow over."

"Finding out the truth isn't worth it?" she asks. "You'd rather make an assumption and live with it than be open to the possibility that you could get what you want, Heathers of the world be damned?"

"Going up against her and all of her friends isn't worth it. Even if she's wrong, she'd make my life hell for turning the tables on her. I'm just going to focus on school like I always do."

My mom retracts her hands and sighs. "Someday, my darling young woman, you're going to learn that things are always more complicated than they seem, and taking the harder path can lead to things you've always hoped for but were too scared to go after."

I roll my eyes at her again. Parents have no idea how vicious seventh-grade girls can be.

"Easy to say when you're not the one who has to deal with it," I grumble. I finish off my cocoa and rise from the table. "Night, Mom."

Mom rises and puts a hand on my arm, stopping me. "I'm serious, Julianna. I know how focused you can be, and how quick you are to shut out things that you can't control. But some of the best things in life are the things we need to believe in enough to fight for. Just don't forget that, okay?"

"Yeah, whatever, Mom."

*She shakes her head and releases me.*

My twelve-year-old self left then, but in my mind now, I hold the picture of my mother close to my heart. The way she used to be. Loving, patient, and always there to guide me. But it's funny, in all these years she's been mentally absent, I haven't allowed myself to remember her like that.

I wonder what she'd say now. Maybe that's exactly what the dream was about. I haven't revisited that particular memory possibly since we had that conversation. But clearly my unconscious brain showed it to me for a reason. It's not rocket science.

I can't control Noah. Not his feelings, not whatever he is or isn't doing. Not what's going on at the hospital. And I get that in a way I'm rejecting him for whatever his reasons are because of all those unknowns, because it's too hard to trust that it'll actually work out. But it's all I know how to do, and it feels like taking back some of the control I've lost. Because choosing him would be a huge leap of faith that he's not exactly what I thought him to be from the start. Even his own actions have been a mixed bag this whole time, and there's enough bad that's come with the good to believe that, despite what I think are good intentions, his interest would lead to anything but heartache. And when there's more doubt than not, life has taught me that it's just not worth the chance.

Unfortunately, my conscious dismissal doesn't easily override my subconscious' nagging, and it takes a good long while, and a lot of tossing and turning, before I'm able to get back to sleep.

* * *

I return to work the next morning, and everyone is as chipper as they have been lately. But on top of my crappy

170

night of unwelcome memories and even crappier sleep, the luster has totally worn off for me.

However, nothing could have prepared me for Dr. Carson's announcement at our morning staff tag-up that, going forward, James Rutherford will be acting as chief hospital director until a replacement is found. Questions shoot around the room as to whether he'll change anything that's already been put in place, but we're reassured he's merely acting as proxy for Noah, who has been called back to the Rutherford Group to handle other emergent issues.

Emergent issues, my ass.

Becca tries all morning to pull me into a conversation about how I'm feeling. But, in all honesty, I'm not sure how to feel. On the one hand, clearly Noah is giving me the space that I asked for. On the other, I wonder if it's just another ploy to manipulate me. Mostly, I hate even thinking about it all.

Becca finally goes to lunch, and I'm enjoying some blissfully quiet and rare time alone at the nurses' station when the last person I expected to see today shows up at the counter.

"Mr. Rutherford," I exclaim, hopping up nervously. "What can I do for you?"

James Rutherford's blue eyes scan me up and down in a way I'm not entirely comfortable with. He's shorter than I thought, and looks even less like his brother than I'd imagined. And while he's still a very good-looking guy, I definitely get a slimy vibe from his mannerisms and the little sneer that looks like it sits permanently on his face.

"You must be Julianna Magnusson," he says in a silky voice.

"That's me," I reply, still confused as to why he's here.

He extends a hand, which I reach over the counter to shake while I make a mental note to bathe in sanitizer tonight.

"I just wanted to meet you," he explains. "Noah said if I can trust anyone here, it's you."

I raise an eyebrow. So. Noah talked to him about me. And naturally, the playboy that he is, James Rutherford wanted to see what all the fuss was about.

"I see," I reply crisply, crossing my arms over my chest. "Well, I'm happy to help in a professional capacity in any way I can." I try not to stress "professional" too hard. "Is there something specific you had in mind, or ..." I trail off, letting the question hang in the air.

"Not at the moment, no," he replies. "But I'll be starting to interview current staff members to see if any are suitable to fill the director's role. I may ask you for your opinion, if that's all right with you?"

I wave a hand, palm up in agreement. "Absolutely, I'd be happy to," I assure him. "Does that mean you won't be interviewing external candidates?"

"That depends," he says with a smirk. "I'd hoped to promote from within so this didn't drag out. Hell, I'd wanted to sell this place off to the highest bidder weeks ago. But now I'm starting to think I might like it around here." His smirk turns toward leering, and I try not to shudder.

And then part of what he said sinks in.

"Wait, I'm sorry, did you say the Rutherford Group had planned to sell this hospital? That's not still a possibility, is it?" I ask, trying not to look as sick as I feel. After everything we've gone through, knowing that was ever a possibility and still might be ... *Calm your tits, Jules*. I take a subtle deep breath, trying not to think myself into a panic attack.

"That was on the table, yes, but don't worry," he replies. "I'm not sure exactly why, but for once my little brother and I didn't see eye to eye. He was dead set on turning things around here. You all should be worshipping the ground he walks on. He stood up to the whole board for this place until he got his way. God knows why, since UCSD Medical offered a fortune to make it their next surgical center. So see that you tell all your little friends not to waste this opportunity, eh?"

My throat tightens. I don't know if it's from knowing that Noah was really going to bat for us the whole time or from James's threat. Either way, the full truth of it hits me. I was so wrong on so many levels. Noah and I may have been at each other's throats constantly, but he was always on my side. On the hospital's side. I've doubted him this whole time for no reason.

Well ... for my own fucked-up reasons. Even my subconscious was trying to tell me to get out of my own way, to let this man in, that he isn't who I thought he was. One offhand comment from James Rutherford and my entire self-delusion that Noah is some sort of master manipulator is shattered. I know I probably only believed it out of self-protection, but still. I'm an idiot.

Meeting James's eyes, I nod mutely, knowing I can't say any of the things going through my head right now.

"Good," he croons. "Well, Miss Magnusson, it was an absolute *pleasure* to meet you. I'll be seeing you again very soon." He winks at me, and I give him the nicest smile I can muster, but I'm sure I still look a little put off. There might not be much hiding how skeezy I find him.

He seems unfazed, though, and responding is totally unnecessary as he heads out of the unit before I can even form a thought.

I slump into my chair and let my head fall to the desk. I squeeze my eyes shut against the tears threatening at the backs of my eyes as I start to realize almost everything bad I thought about Noah may have had more to do with my own bullshit.

"Whatcha doin'?" Becca's chipper voice breaks through my little pity party.

My head snaps up to find her coming around the counter and giving me a weird look.

I shake my head and bite my lip, still not sure if I can trust myself to talk. Becca instantly gets that something must have happened because she sets her purse down on the spot and rushes to wrap her arms around me.

"Oh, boo, you okay? Tell me what happened," she urges, stroking my back gently.

For some reason, it makes me laugh. She looks at me like I've lost my marbles, and it makes me laugh even harder. Because I have lost my marbles. I chased off the perfect guy because I couldn't see past the labels I'd put on him. On us.

"Okay, Jules, you're starting to freak me out here," she cautions, pulling back.

I shake my head and wipe my eyes.

"Sorry," I say, finally finding my voice. "I've just been a complete fucking idiot, that's all."

Becca arches an eyebrow and puts her hands on her hips.

"I will not have you talking about one of my favorite people that way," she reprimands me.

"You're sweet," I say drily. And then I proceed to tell her about my conversation with James. And how everyone was right — I thought I knew everything. But what I didn't know was that Noah was never the enemy, and what a complete fool I feel like.

"You're right," she says after I've finished. "You're a complete fucking idiot."

I swat at her playfully. "You're not supposed to agree with me," I tease.

She rolls her eyes hard. "Girl, I call it like I see it. You mistook chemistry for animosity. Sounds like you two can't be in a room without getting each other all worked up. And if you don't let it out between the sheets, what did you expect to happen? Honestly. You're usually way smarter than this, Jules," she admonishes.

I cover my eyes with my hands. "Gooooooodddd, I hate it when you're right," I moan. I drop my hands. "What do I do, Becks? The man declared his love for me, and I shat all over it. I don't think there's any coming back from that."

Becca blanches. "He did what, now?"

My eyes widen. "I … may have forgotten to tell you about that part," I admit sheepishly.

"Well?" she demands, smacking a hand on the desk.

"You know, we probably have patients to see or something —"

"The short version, then," she insists.

I heave a deep sigh. I summarize it for her as best I can, feeling stupider and stupider with each sentence. "So yeah, he basically told me he loved me, got my parents' care paid for, and then I told him he was trying to buy me off. Then, come to find out, he's been going against his family to try to save this hospital, probably only because I wanted him to. So, you're right. I'm a complete fucking idiot."

"Good. So you realize he was probably doing all that *because* he loves you, right? Not to get you to love him?" she pushes.

I press my lips together. It's all too much truth to handle at once.

"Stop being right," I holler at her.

We both crack up laughing.

"Yeah, okay, I'll leave you alone now," she agrees. "But I trust you're not going to just let this go, yeah?"

"Yeah," I agree with a smile. "And I think I know just what I need to do to fix it."

# CHAPTER 19

I send Noah a text message and coordinate a meeting at the office he'd been using upstairs just after my shift. Thankfully, he doesn't ask many questions, probably assuming I'm going to give him a hard time for switching things up with his brother without any warning.

I finish a little early and use the staff showers to clean up and change into a set of street clothes I keep in my locker for emergencies. I pull out my hairband and let my auburn waves tumble down my back. I'd rather be fresh and prepared for our conversation, rather than smelling like hospital and wearing rumpled scrubs. It's just a simple pair of jeans and a purple V-neck tee, but it's cute enough to give me the confidence I'm going to need.

Still, when I head upstairs close to six-thirty, I'm nervous as all hell. It doesn't help that when I approach the door, I can hear two voices inside. It only takes a moment to realize that James and Noah are both in there. While I can't hear what they're saying, the conversation sounds heated.

I hover a few feet from the door, unsure of whether I should approach. I'm spared deciding when the door flies open and James comes stomping out.

He gives me a curt nod but says nothing as he passes. With wide eyes, I carefully approach the now-open door. I peer in and Noah is pacing, running his hands through his hair, when he catches sight of me. He abruptly stops and smooths his rumpled sky-blue dress shirt.

"Come in, Julianna," he says, sounding tired.

I slip inside, gently closing the door behind me. When I turn back, Noah is seated behind the desk, an eyebrow cocked at the door.

"We need to talk," I say by way of explanation.

He presses his lips together, gesturing to the chair across the desk from him. He looks ridiculously stressed out.

I slink into the chair without protest, folding my hands together in my lap nervously.

"I hope I wasn't the cause of any friction between you and your brother," I say quietly.

Noah leans forward on those gorgeous forearms of his, shaking his head. "Not really. There's always been friction between James and me."

"Except, you disagreed with him because of me, didn't you?" I press. "About keeping Rutherford Hospital?"

He looks up in shock. "He wasn't supposed to tell you that. But yes, more or less. I didn't do it to buy your —"

I hold a hand up. "I know," I interject. "I know, Noah. You did so much without ever being asked. I doubted you from the start, and I was wrong. There was just so much tension, and things were already difficult here." I shake my head, stopping myself. "I didn't ask you here to make excuses."

"So why did you ask me here?"

I look up into his eyes. "To apologize. I'm sorry, Noah. I'm sorry I made this harder on you. I'm sorry I didn't trust you. But most of all, I'm sorry I believed you would ever try to buy my love."

He pushes out a dramatic sigh and leans back in his chair. "Thank you for saying that," he replies. Then he looks back up to meet my gaze. "From the moment you told me your story in that office outside of that ballroom, all I've wanted to do was help you. And that both intrigued me and totally freaked me out. Because that's not usually how I operate." He pauses, his eyes glassy. "I tried to ignore it. I decided in that moment to let it be, that it was just because I was so fucking attracted to you. But I couldn't get it out of my head after that. I couldn't get *you* out of my head." He huffs a breath out of his nose. "And now I sound like a total stalker."

A small laugh bubbles out of me. "Better a stalker than an idiot," I say. "Because that's exactly what I've been. I'm so stupid. I was totally blinded by my own biases. You may be Warren Rutherford's son, but you're also so much more than that. You're fair. And kind. And so generous." I look up at the ceiling, blinking away my tears. "I'm so sorry, Noah. Truly. So, so sorry. I was so very wrong about you."

I hear the rustle of fabric, but I don't trust myself to look. To not cry. I feel him approach, settling next to me.

"Look at me, Julianna," he says, his voice soft but commanding. And as always, I can't resist it, and my eyes meet his as he's knelt next to me. His large, strong hands wrap around mine and he lifts them to his mouth, placing a gentle kiss there. "Everything I did was to make things better for you, easier. Whether you knew it or not. Hell, whether you *ever* knew it or not. It took me weeks to admit how fucking in love with you I was from that very first night. And if my money is what's keeping us apart, I'd give up every goddamn penny if it meant getting to be with you. I've never cared about the money. Not like I care about you."

My eyes fill with tears. "But I was so awful to you, Noah," I whisper. I close my eyes and shake my head. "How could you love me? All I did was make things harder."

I feel his hand cup my cheek, and I open my eyes to see him smiling. "Your feistiness is what drew me to you. And if you haven't realized it yet, we Rutherfords do love a good argument. And I'd rather argue with you than be alone with my piles of money."

I sniff and laugh. "You don't really have piles of money laying around, do you?" I ask skeptically.

He laughs. "No, I don't," he admits. "I was making a point. But I like that you felt the need to bust my chops anyway."

I chew on my lips to suppress my smile. "Does that mean you'll come back to work here?" I ask.

He gives me a surprised look. "If you want me to, yes, I can," he replies. "But if it's all the same, I'd rather not." A hurt look flits across my face, but he shakes his head, stopping my reaction in its tracks. "It's tough, being here, not touching you. That's all."

"I know how you feel," I admit. "It used to make me so angry that I found you so attractive."

"Really?" he says in a teasing tone. "Because you hid it so well."

I wrinkle my nose and shake my head at him. "Laugh it up, chuckles," I tease back, rising from my chair. "If this is how you're going to treat me, I'll just be going then." I turn to make for the door. As I hoped, he grabs my wrist, turning me back toward him.

"Oh, no, you don't," he growls, pulling me into his arms. He looks down into my eyes, his warm, honeyed irises trained on my face. "Tell me we can give this a shot."

I press my palms against his hard chest. "On one condition," I reply.

"I'm listening."

A feline grin splits my face. "I want you to take me on your desk. Right now."

His pupils dilate, but he doesn't move an inch. "Well, shit," he huffs. "Do you now?"

I smile beatifically up at him, wrapping my arms around his neck.

"I do," I confirm. "Because you have my trust Noah, and my respect." I pause, emotions rising in me that I've forbidden myself for so long. "And my love."

His hands tighten on my waist.

"Say it again," he begs, closing his eyes.

I bite into my bottom lip and smile, rising on my toes until my mouth hovers near his.

"I love you, Noah Rutherford," I whisper.

His lips crash against mine, his strong arms wrapping around me until I'm pressed tight against his chest as his tongue teases at my lips. I open to him, and our mouths dance for a moment before he breaks away, spinning me around in his arms.

His lips caress my neck as his hands work my breasts. His fingers trail down my stomach and to the button on my jeans. He pulls back slightly, his eyes locked on mine.

"Make no mistake," he says clearly. "I'm going to take you home after we're done here and we're going to set another orgasm record. But right now, I'm going to bend you over this desk and fuck you like I've been dreaming about for weeks."

I arch at his words. "God, yes, please," I moan. I grab one of his hands with mine, using it to stroke me through my jeans.

He nips roughly at my neck as he goes back to undoing my buttons, then with a rough tug he's got my jeans and panties pulled down to my thighs. A few scoots forward and my legs hit the desk. I lean forward obligingly, putting my bare ass on display for him. I thought I'd be self-conscious getting down and dirty at work, but it's *thrilling*. And so much more of a turn-on than I ever thought it would be.

He runs a hand down my backside, then between my legs. The noise he makes when he feels how wet I am just makes me more so. And the sound of his zipper lowering nearly sends me over the edge.

I look back to find him fisting his cock and looking at me from under hooded eyelids.

"Just so you know," he says, "this has already blown the fantasy out of the water. You're fucking perfect, Julianna." He rubs his bare cock between my legs, asking for permission. I nod eagerly, already knowing we're both safe. He eases the tip in, and I gasp. Much to my dismay, that makes him pull back out. "You're going to have to be quiet, baby." I nod and whimper, and an instant later he rewards me by burying himself swiftly to the hilt.

I have to choke back my moan, closing my eyes and pressing my forehead into the desktop to cope with how fucking good it feels. How much I missed having him inside of me.

"You okay?" he asks quietly and tenderly.

I look back at him. "So good," I breathe softly. "Don't stop."

His eyes darken and he swings his hips, expertly pounding me with just the right amount of force to fuck me hard yet somehow keep from moving the furniture or making any noise but the low sound of skin on skin. It's beyond erotic, and each thrust sends me soaring.

I reach back, needing to touch him, needing to hold onto him to withstand the pleasure without screaming my head off. His hand reaches out and grips mine. What I didn't realize was that would give him more leverage to fuck me harder.

"Oh, god," I moan a little louder than I intended. I bite into my lip. "I'm gonna come."

His only answer is to fuck me even harder, which sends me spiraling over the edge. I somehow manage to come silently, and it just makes the orgasm that much more intense. My body is so tight, my sex squeezing down so hard, that I feel, rather than hear, Noah join me in his own orgasm.

I slump face first onto the desk as I catch my breath.

Noah's hands caress my hips and he leans forward, placing a kiss on my lower back where my shirt has ridden up.

"I'm going to pull out now," he warns.

I take a deep breath, then nod. When he slips out, I lean up and shimmy quickly back into my pants, knowing I can change as soon as I'm home. Which will hopefully be very, very soon. Likewise, he zips up, righting his clothing and hair as much as possible.

"That was …" I trail off, having no words for exactly how fantastic that was.

He pulls me back into his arms. "Just the beginning," he murmurs, looking down into my eyes.

"My place?" I ask breathily.

"I'll race you there," he teases.

I give him an assessing look, not sure if he's serious. But probably best we leave separately anyway. So with the quickest of pecks on the lips, I snatch my purse off the chair and hightail it out of the room. His laughter follows me down the hall.

* * *

Much later that night, after several more rounds of mind-blowing sex, Noah lies next to me in my bed, running his fingers lazily through my hair.

"Did you mean it?" I ask, running my own fingers along his taut abdomen.

"Mean what?" he asks sounding happy and tired.

I prop myself up to look into his eyes.

"That you'd give it all up," I remind him.

"The money?" he asks, to which I nod. He scoots up on the pillow. "Of course. I can donate it to the Alzheimer's Foundation. I can always make more. It's just money."

"You don't have to, not really," I finally reply. "I guess I just have a hard time wrapping my head around both having that much money and being so willing to part with it."

Noah considers that for a minute. "We had very different upbringings," he allows. "But it really is just money. And you're right, it can't buy love. But it *can* help you do some amazing things for the people you love. While it's not everything, I enjoy being able to do those kinds of things." He looks down at me. "Everyone has different resources at their disposal. Some people have a talent for making money. Some a talent for healing." He gives me a meaningful smile. "I might as well use my talent to do good in this world. Money, like everything, is just a tool. It's not inherently good or bad. It's how you use it that defines you."

"Wow," I whisper. "That's … well, I can't argue with that."

Noah chuckles. "How about this? How about you help me make sure I'm using my money to help people instead of being a stuck-up rich guy who blows it on cars and vacation houses and other stuff that doesn't really matter."

I smile up at him. "On one condition."

"You and your conditions," he grumbles in a teasing tone. "Go on."

"You keep the hot air balloon," I reply.

That gets a full-throated laugh from him. "Absolutely," he agrees. "Though I'd argue that the hot air balloon definitely helped me knock your socks off. So worth every penny in my book."

I roll my eyes and smack him playfully. "I'd argue, but you're not wrong. Though I was kind of thinking we could use it for therapy? Because it's such a spectacular experience, yet so chill and it doesn't have to last very long. It might be the perfect thing for some of the patients at my parents' nursing home. Something like that could go a long way toward improving the lives of people who are sick, lonely, and scared."

Noah's expression softens, and he flips me over onto my back, holding himself over me on his forearms.

"You're amazing," he murmurs, looking down at me. "I love you, Julianna."

I look up at him, unable to believe that we're here, finally. Getting over my own stupid notions of what someone like him should be like was the best thing I ever did.

"I love you too, Noah," I admit.

His mouth reaches down for mine, his lips tenderly caressing me. After a moment, he pushes off of me, climbing off the bed and pulling his briefs on.

I roll onto my side with a frown. "You're staying, right?" I ask, suddenly self-conscious.

He looks back at me and grins. "I'm just going to get a glass of water. Want one?"

I let out a sigh of relief, not sure where my sudden bout of nerves came from. "Yes, please," I reply.

He gives me a funny look, then comes back to the bed, leaning over and kissing me deeply.

"Don't worry," he assures me, looking intently into my eyes. "Now that I've got you, I'm not going anywhere. So you'd better get used to having me around."

I can't help the grin that spreads across my face.

"Promise?" I ask, batting my eyelashes at him.

He runs a thumb over my cheek. "I promise," he replies with a wink. "And you can take *that* to the bank."

I tip my head back and laugh. "Are you always this cheesy?" I tease.

He straightens up and smirks down at me. "Only for you, baby. Only for you."

As he walks away, chuckling, I sink back into the bed, happier than I can ever remember being. More in love than I can ever remember being. More hopeful than I can ever remember being.

As different as we are, I have to admit to myself that we just work. That Becca was right — there's a tension between us that's like a thread pulling us together. Fighting against it just hurt us both. But giving in to it? Nothing has ever felt this right.

I wasn't wrong; you can't buy love. But you also can't help who you fall in love with. You just have to be able to let yourself see them for who they really are, not just who you see them as. It's hard, getting past your own perceptions, past the hurts that scar you along the way. But I think that's the real lesson in life: being willing to revisit your assumptions before they keep you from living happily ever after.

*Will* I live happily ever after with Noah? It's early days, but I can see it happening. At least now I know I'm not standing in the way of my own happiness. And that feels pretty fucking amazing.

# A NOTE FROM THE AUTHOR

If you enjoyed this book, I would greatly appreciate if you would take a few moments to leave a review, even if it's just a sentence or two saying that you like the book and why. Reviews are valuable feedback that let both the author and other readers know that the book is an enjoyable read. When you leave a positive review it also lets the vendor know that the book is worth promoting, as the more reviews a book receives, the more they will recommend it to other readers. Regardless, thank you for reading this book, and for your support!

# ACKNOWLEDGEMENTS

It takes a village to write a book. I'm especially thankful for mine this time around.

Big thanks to my beautiful betas, Lindsey, Erin, Jacquie — you ladies make my stories better and cheer me on with equal grace.

Permanent thanks to my editor-slash-BFF, Jenny. I miss you to Planet Spaceball and back.

Many thanks to my sensational street team, the Romance Reader Squad. I couldn't ask for a more supportive team of readers.

And a huge thank you to all my readers — I'm so humbled that you take the time to read my words.

Thank you also to the Instagram author community, my Badass Author Babes in particular, whose wealth of knowledge and depth of love and support is endless.

Find your village, love them hard, and read and share naughty romance. Definitely a recipe for happiness!

BTW, I'd thank my husband, but he stopped reading my books a while ago. Guess he's not into book boyfriends (thank goodness for that!).

Haven't read the first Life Lessons Novel with Sasha and Cal's story? Check out

*NEVER DATE A DOCTOR*

Read on for a sneak peek!

# CHAPTER 1

"So what's it going to take, Sasha?" Becca asks pointedly before taking another sip of coffee.

I shoot her a pointed grimace. "I'm not asking for fucking Henry Cavill," I grouse. "Is it really too much to want a good, steady guy who treats me well but also makes my toes curl and my lady bits swoon when I see him?"

She arches an eyebrow and thinks about that as she continues to drink her coffee. Way too slowly for the small break we're allotted. I tap my fingers impatiently next to my empty coffee cup. Finally, she finishes and sets hers on the peeling laminate tabletop.

"Yes," she says flatly, rising to rinse her cup. "Because the type of guy who curls *your* toes is going to know he's hot shit. And that doesn't exactly translate to boyfriend material."

"Oh? And what exactly is my *type*?" I rise from my chair, setting my coffee mug back in its usual spot without rinsing it. Lord knows I'm going to be back in here for another cup soon anyway.

"'Henry Cavill' says it all, my dear," she replies airily as she heads back into the main office. "Tall, dark, handsome, blue eyes, rockin' bod. *Your type.* You set your standards too damn high and you're stuck in a no-dating rut."

I frown deeply as I approach the intake station and grab the chart slotted into my cubby. I'm not exactly in a position to argue, as she's not wrong. But having it pointed out so bluntly is beyond annoying. Just because I hold out for my "type" doesn't mean I'm hopelessly stuck.

"It's called having standards," I respond drily. "I can define that if it's unclear."

"So are you ever going to tell me *why* that's a type you can't seem to break away from?" she teases, totally ignoring my not-so-subtle dig as she settles in at the nurses' station. Her eyes suddenly widen. "Oh god, that's not what your dad looks like, is it?"

My eyes flick up from the chart in my hands.

"Becca, that's disgusting." I gesture to my dark blond hair. "Besides, where do you think I got this?"

She shrugs and grins mischievously. "Good. Because daddy issues are a whole other ballgame. So who was it? First boyfriend? First lay? Both?" Her eyebrows waggle suggestively.

This time I slam the folder closed. "Christ, Becks, keep your voice down." My eyes dart around, hoping nobody else heard her.

"Oh, this must be good, you little prude, you," she says, greedily rubbing her hands together.

"I'm not a *prude*," I protest. "I just don't talk about my sex life at work. Or jump into bed with every guy I date." I shoot her a meaningful, if not teasing, stare.

"Maybe you should give it a try sometime. It's every bit as fun as it sounds," she retorts with a wink. "Fine, have it your way. Go to your ten a.m., but we're having drinks after work, and I *am* getting this story."

"Have it your way," I reply mockingly, "just so long as you're buying."

"I think I will have it my way, thank you very much," she replies airily. But then her eyes go wide as she looks over my shoulder.

I turn to see the chief of our unit headed at us, a stern frown on his grey-bearded face. He's always in a shit mood, and I know I need to get in to see my patient before I become his next target.

"Dr. MacDougall is all you, Becks," I whisper with a sly grin before shooting into exam room seven. I just catch her annoyed glare as I close the door behind me.

* * *

"I swear. I love my job, but if one more old man tries to feel me up while I'm doing an echo, I'm going to respond with violence." I take a huge gulp of the martini in front of me, knowing even that won't wash away the memory of his wrinkled paw squeezing my ass.

Becca shoots me a sympathetic look from across the small table we're perched at. It barely fits our drinks, and the place is packed, but I guess I should've realized that, as it's a Friday night. I just don't pay much attention to the days of the week anymore, unless it's a school night. The hazards of working at a cardiac unit that's open seven days a week while going to school to graduate from nurse to nurse-practitioner. My days have two classifications: non-school days that are just long and difficult, and school days which are so grueling they could be considered a form of torture. Christ, I'm such a masochist.

"Been there," Becca agrees. "But honestly, I wouldn't have even minded. It's been way too long since I've had *any* action."

I laugh incredulously. "I find that hard to believe."

She shrugs. "Oh, believe it. Even I go through dry spells. And you know what they say about desperate times …" She looks around at the crowds wistfully before her eyes wander back to mine. "If only there were anyone here worth going after. But we have other business to get to anyway. Now. About Henry Cavill."

"What about him? Did you want to go see a movie after this?" I dodge jokingly.

One of Becca's perfectly shaped eyebrows lifts. I throw up my hands in defeat.

"Fine. But you're going to make fun of me."

"*Moi*? I would never." The evil glint in her eye belies her innocent tone. "Seriously, though, out with it. I'm on a mission here to get us both laid."

"Getting laid isn't really an issue," I reply with a shrug. At five-and-a-half feet, with blond hair and curves in all the right places, attracting male attention has never been a problem. The opposite, in fact, especially working in the medical profession. Though frankly I think just being female is enough, since I know most of the other nurses and MAs at work have to deal with the same crap. You'd think it was still 1950, not 2020, the way some of these old bastards behave. And in a facility that deals exclusively with heart problems, we pretty much get mostly elderly patients.

"So out with it," Becca prompts. "Maybe we can cleanse you of your need for Superman."

I stick my tongue out at her, and she laughs.

"Fine," I reply with a sigh. "But if I tell you, you have to promise not to laugh."

Becca presses her lips together in amusement and gestures for me to continue, twirling her dark brown hair around a finger while her equally dark brown eyes survey me. We've worked together at the cardiac unit for too many years — she was already a medical assistant when I started there during nursing school — and have been friends just as long, so she knows me better than almost anybody. But this ... this, I've never told *anyone*.

I down the rest of my drink. What the hell. Here goes.

"When I was fourteen, I went to my first airshow sans parents," I begin. Becca grins widely. I don't have to explain the significance of that to her; she grew up in San Diego too, attending the annual airshow just the same as I always have. Ogling the hot guys on offer, in uniform and out. Going on your own meant the chance to flirt unimpeded by parental units.

"So, your Henry was a hunky sailor, huh?" she teases.

I shrug. "I don't know," I reply honestly. "He wasn't in uniform. We didn't even speak. My friends were pulling me toward the hangar, and I looked up and there he was. He was with a group of guys heading the other direction."

I close my eyes, bringing up the mental picture that hasn't faded in detail, despite it being ten years ago.

"He was older than me, maybe late teens? But he had dark-brown hair and the most beautiful, clear blue eyes I'd ever seen. Seriously, when we locked eyes, I froze in place. I couldn't move. He was so gorgeous. So fucking perfect. But mostly ..." I open my eyes to see Becca staring, enraptured.

"What?" she prompts impatiently.

I scrunch up my nose. In for a penny ...

"I felt *it*," I admit on a sigh. "A tug in my chest. Like the world dropped away, and it was just us. Like the universe went quiet so I could hear the pounding of my heart. Feel the connection between us like it was a living thing." I lean back, lamenting my empty glass. "And then my friends pulled me away and I lost him in the crowd."

Becca sits up straight, her face dropping.

"That's it? You saw some guy during fleet week ten years ago who got your hormones going and you're spoiled for anyone who doesn't have dark hair and blue eyes? Fuck, Sash, that's nuts."

"And that's me, done for the night," I reply, rising from my seat.

She reaches out and grabs my hand, pulling me back as I retreat. "I'm sorry," she replies. "Please, stay. I'll even buy you another drink."

A small smile finds its way onto my lips, and I sink back into the chair.

"You're forgiven. But I swear I'm not crazy. I don't think I date guys who look like that because of him. I think that's just what I find attractive. But what I can't seem to find is something that moves me the way looking into his eyes did." I pause, trying to figure out how to explain it. I look back up, and Becca is staring at me curiously. "It was like … seeing a stranger, but knowing everything about him was just there, waiting for me to know. And everything in me *wanted* that, wanted to know him. Like it would be the answer to everything." I can tell by the look on her face that she totally doesn't get where I'm coming from, so I just stop, shaking my head.

"I can't say I understand," she replies slowly. "But that's cool. I mean, I get wanting to really feel something with someone. But I guess I didn't realize you were such a fucking romantic."

I laugh at Becca's talent for keeping things from getting too serious. "I'm really not. It was just a thing that happened. But it's always stuck in my head. Like that's the way it should be. That's how I should feel when I meet the right guy."

"So that's why you've only had a handful of relationships that never lasted longer than a few months the whole time I've known you?"

"I don't know. I guess I always chalked that up to focusing on school, and my career. And, I mean, I'm only twenty-four. But I guess, yeah, I've never really felt that again. I'm not stupid, though, Becks. It's not like I don't give guys a chance. Even if there's not that initial spark. I try to stick around, waiting for it. But it never comes."

"Wow," Becca mouths.

"Have you ever felt that way?" I ask, suddenly wondering if something is wrong with me.

"I've been attracted to guys. Wanted to jump their bones. Well, actually jumped their bones," she allows. "But I can't say I've ever had my *universe go quiet*."

"Fuck you, Becca. Fuck you." Becca, thankfully, is extremely difficult to offend, and she just laughs in response.

"You wish," she jokes with a wink. "You know I don't swing that way."

"Me neither. But wouldn't that just solve both of our problems," I tease back with my own wink.

# CHAPTER 2

The next morning I fill my coffee mug to the brim and stifle a yawn as I head into our mandated morning staff tag-up. Becca joins me as I pass the nurses' station, cradling her own giant cup of java.

"Someday," she sighs, "I'll have a job where I don't have to be in at six a.m. on a Saturday. I wonder what MacDougall wants, anyway."

"There's a new doc on the block," a cheery voice comes from behind us.

We both look back to see my supervisor, Julianna Magnusson, approaching, looking every inch the morning person she is, all bright-eyed with a pep in her step. Well, supervisor, mentor, and friend. None of us would make it without Jules. She's been a nurse practitioner at Rutherford Hospital for ten years and was a nurse here for six before that. She knows more than just about anyone at the hospital how things run across units. Which also makes her privy to the best gossip.

"Yeah? Any dirt?" Becca asks gleefully as Jules joins us.

Jules sweeps her burgundy hair into a ponytail with a quiet smile. "Only that he's coming from Cedars-Sinai in L.A., where he also apparently did his cardiac surgery training." Becca gives her a disappointed look and Jules laughs. "Sorry, babes, I bumped into Dr. MacDougall and that was all he had time to tell me. We're all about to find out anyway."

Becca gives an indifferent shrug, clearly having wanted to know before everyone else, and Jules and I share a look as we enter the staff meeting room. We seem to be the last in, aside from Dr. MacDougall and our new addition. Becca sniffs the air suspiciously.

"Oh god, what is it?" I ask. In a hospital, you never know what an odd smell is going to lead to.

Becca takes another deep sniff and her eyes go wide. "Donuts!" And she's off, dragging me across the room to where, behind a cluster of MAs, there are, in fact, two huge boxes of donuts.

"Damn, Becks, you're a freaking bloodhound," I tease as she grabs the nearest donut and stuffs it in her face.

"Oh my god, they're still warm," she groans around a mouthful of pastry.

"You're a nutjob," I say with a laugh.

"Good morning, everybody," Dr. MacDougall's voice booms from behind me.

I spin in place at his clear call to order. As the room quiets, my eyes fall on our chief … and a man I've never seen before standing next to him. It takes my brain about two seconds when a loud gasp of recognition escapes me. Everyone turns to look, including him, and I blush deeply. Thankfully, Dr. MacDougall clears his throat, bringing the attention back to the front of the room. As he starts his usual greeting speech, Becca leans in.

"What was that all about?" she whispers.

I turn toward her so she can see the shock on my face, and my hand finds hers, gripping it tightly.

"It's *him*," I hiss. Becca gives me a confused look, and I roll my eyes. "*Universe Guy.*"

Becca gives me a skeptical look, her eyes turning back to the front. Taking in what I did. All six-feet-two-ish inches of the dark-haired, blue-eyed, and unquestionably sexy hunk of a well-built man in blue scrubs and a white lab coat standing next to Dr. MacDougall as he rambles about our round stats for the week.

"Are you sure?" she whispers back. "Maybe you just *think* it's Universe Guy because we were just talking about him."

With a lump in my throat, I chance another look at him. Thankfully, his eyes are roaming the crowd as Dr. MacDougall gives his usual boring speech that is now shifting toward a lecture on proper chart notes. The young man I remember was clean-shaven, and though this guy has a well-trimmed beard that defines his sharp jaw, otherwise it's the exact face I remember, just a bit older. Same broad shoulders. Same trim waist. Though he's filled out in the chest and arms, and I can practically see the muscles straining against the fabric of his shirt. But I've got the same butterflies in my stomach.

"I don't know. I'm pretty sure it's him," I mumble. As if he heard me, his eyes land on me. And the sound of Dr. MacDougall droning on muffles under the pounding of my heart in my ears. My insides tighten. And, for the second time in my life, the universe goes quiet. A surge of emotion pounds through me, even stronger than the one ten years ago. I've never reacted to anyone this way, and it's equal parts terrifying and thrilling, and I can't stop staring back into his baby blues.

But when his eyes snap away suddenly, the volume comes rushing back. And I notice that my heart is pounding and I'm breathing like I just ran sprints. I take a deep breath to steady myself, hoping nobody noticed my ridiculous reaction to him.

"… and so, finally, I'd like to introduce the newest addition to our team, specializing in cardiac surgery, Dr. Thompson. Though he was heavily recruited out of his residency with Cedars-Sinai, he chose to stay there — until now. We are extremely lucky to have him, so please join me in welcoming him to our team."

A smattering of applause rings around the room, and I clap my hands together with them, but I'm completely numb with shock.

Dr. Thompson puts a hand up in greeting, and the room once again falls silent.

"Thank you, everyone," he says. And my jaw drops at the unmistakably posh British accent. "I'm Dr. Caleb Thompson. As you've probably noticed, I'm not originally from Los Angeles." A few in the crowd, mostly females, titter at his comment. "I graduated from Cambridge seven years ago now, then moved to the States for my residency. While I enjoyed my time at Cedars-Sinai, I'm already very impressed with Rutherford Hospital, and I'm pleased to be working with you all. I will be making my rounds to get to know each of you throughout the day. But first, may I ask, who are my surgical nurses?" Jules' hand goes up, as do several others. "Excellent. Good to put faces to the names on my sheet." He holds a clipboard aloft with a smile that gets another few titters from the peanut gallery. But my heart is in my shoes.

He moved here seven years ago. He can't be Universe Guy. My eyes scan his face as he continues to talk about how he plans to integrate into established routines, consultations, and the like, but all I can think about is how much he looks like The Guy. I even had the same reaction.

And then some. By the time he's done and we've all been dismissed, I'm dumbly zoning out in my own bubble of confusion.

I feel a tug on my elbow as Becca tries to get my attention.

"Hey, I have to start processing patients. You okay?" I finally look up to see the look of pity on her face. She's clearly also realized he can't possibly be the same guy from my story.

"Sure, yeah," I mumble. "Sorry. I just could've sworn it was him."

Becca gives a light shrug. "Probably better that it isn't," she says gently. "After all, what's the first rule of Nurses' Club?"

That gets a smile out of me. "Never talk about Nurses' Club?" I tease.

She wrinkles her nose and jiggles her head. "That just gets funnier every time I hear it," she replies wryly, then gives me an expectant look.

"I know, I know," I reply with a sigh. "Never date a doctor."

It's been drilled into me so many times. Not because it's against policy; it's not. But the relationship between doctors and their support staff is already difficult at best, and lives are literally on the line every day. Even in my time here, I see the wisdom of not complicating that further. Not that it matters. Even if he was Universe Guy, what chance would I have with a guy like that?

"That's right, boo," Becca says. "Chin up." She shoots a look at Dr. Thompson, who is deep in conversation with Jules. "If it helps, there are still donuts left."

A little chuckle escapes me, and it snaps me back to reality. What am I even doing thinking about this guy?

He's not who I thought he was. He's now a doctor in our unit. Even if he was interested, it's *not* going to happen. And while I hadn't been planning on having one, I decide a donut sounds pretty damn good.

"It does help," I reply with a grateful smile. "Thanks, Becks. See you in a bit."

She gives me a wink and slips out the door. I grab the last glazed donut and follow suit, not even looking at Dr. Hottie on my way out. It's better that way, because I have a feeling being too close to him wouldn't go well for me.

But Jules apparently has other ideas.

"Sasha," she calls as I step over the threshold, "come meet Dr. Thompson."

I turn slowly on the spot to find Jules staring at me expectantly. Dr. Thompson is looking at me, a half-smile on his face as he studies me curiously. His eyes sweeping casually over me sends chills down my spine.

"Of course," I reply, clearing my throat and switching the donut to my left hand so I can extend my right as I step toward them. "It's a pleasure to meet you, Dr. Thompson."

His large, warm hand slips into mine, and my insides do their little clenching thing again. He may not be who I thought he was, but, as Becca teased me about on Friday, I have a type. And he's definitely it. I swallow hard and try not to let the nervous tension I feel affect my smile as I look up into his eyes. It doesn't work, and I push back against the well of want that is bubbling up inside of me.

"Sasha … Suvorin?" he guesses.

I clear my throat, willing back my body's reaction. "You're a quick study," I reply.

His answering laugh is warm and rich, and does nothing to help me forget how attractive he is. "I am a doctor. We pretty much just memorize things for a living." I'd like to respond, but for a moment all I can think is, *Damn, that accent is sexy as hell*. His hand lingers in mine for a little longer than is strictly necessary. Jules looks between us both, and I withdraw my hand self-consciously.

"I have some experience with that. I'm working toward my master's in nursing, and it's pretty much the same," I finally reply, finding myself again.

His eyebrows jump and a slow smile spreads across his lips. I can't help but stare, noting his bottom lip is fuller than the top. I watch him tuck it into his mouth, the hair under the center of his lip moving with it. It's undeniably sexy.

"Ah, yes, getting your MSN? That's lovely," he replies. And the way he says "lovely," I know I'm going to be repeating it to myself in his accent for the rest of the morning. "So I don't detect a Russian accent, despite the surname ..."

I smile tolerantly. I get that a lot. To the extent of actual strangers full on speaking to me in Russian like I should understand. "My grandparents came here many years ago, and my parents preferred we speak English at home so I didn't have any trouble at school. I'm afraid I know about as much Russian as Jules here."

Jules smiles at me right as Dr. Franklin, one of our cardiologists, pops into the room. "Cal, my first consult is here. Join me?"

Dr. Thompson — or Cal, apparently — gives him a sharp nod.

"I expect I'll be seeing you both around," he says to Jules and me.

"Of course," Jules pipes chirpily.

"Yes, nice meeting you," I reply softly, but he's already headed out the door. Thank god. I finally relax, the weird pull he has on my hormones now absent.

Jules fans herself dramatically. "Is it hot in here or was it just him?" she gushes. "Whew! And he seems so *nice*. Definitely trouble with a capital T, that one."

My gut twinges unpleasantly, and I turn to toss the donut in the garbage, having completely lost my appetite.

"He seems okay," I say with a shrug.

Jules smirks at me knowingly. "Oh please, if eye contact was a sex act, you two would've just gotten to third base."

"He's too old for me," I protest. Or at least, I assume he is.

Jules snorts as she heads out the door, so I follow along. "He's about my age," she scoffs. "And I'm only ten years older than you. That's no biggie."

"Except he's a doctor, and —"

"Yeah, yeah, yeah, never date a doctor. I practically invented that rule, Sasha. And do you know why?"

I look up at her, since she's a good four inches taller than me, not sure if this is a trap. "Why?"

"Because I've dated enough doctors to know better."

"Precisely," I respond. "So it doesn't matter how old he is. It's not like either of us is going to date him."

Jules cackles. "No, Sasha, *I've* dated enough doctors to know better. That's part of the fun of having rules: breaking them to find out why they're rules in the first place."

I shoot her a concerned look as we approach the supply closet. "I'm not sure how I feel about someone responsible for so many people's lives on a daily basis having that kind of attitude," I tease. Well, mostly tease. Jules is usually one of the most cautious people I know, so I find this reversal oddly confusing.

She waves a hand at me as we start prepping our supplies for the day.

"You know I would never endanger a patient. I'm not talking about that. I'm talking about you," she replies seriously, maintaining firm but kind eye contact as she mechanically sorts syringes. "You're so serious, so focused. If someone catches your eye, don't write them off because of a rule that's not even really a rule. You never know. That's all I'm saying."

I raise an eyebrow. "I happen to like focusing on things that really matter," I reply archly. "Ever since I started volunteering at this hospital as a teenager, I've always known this is what I wanted to do. I like focusing on it." And not getting distracted by ridiculously hot doctors.

"I know, Sash," she says, handing me a stack of dressing gowns. "Just don't be so focused that you miss out on other opportunities that are part of the human experience." She winks at me, and I find myself a little aggravated. I may not be the most social person, but I've dated. I've gotten out. I mean, not exactly frequently these days, but she's talking like I'm eschewing men and I need to drop everything to go after this one because we made some flirty eye contact. She doesn't need to know about the other stuff, it would just encourage her.

So instead of arguing, I just shake my head and wheel the stocked cart away, intent on focusing on what I always focus on: my job.

It's not long before Becca catches up with me, as I'm cleaning instruments in the sterilization area.

"Hey, Dr. C is looking for you," she tells me.

I raise an eyebrow. Dr. Carson is my least favorite cardiologist on the unit. He's *extremely* particular about how his exam rooms are set up and shoves most of his work off on the nurses regularly. Not that that's terribly unusual, it's just extra annoying because of his attitude.

"Gee, well, I'll just jump right over then," I reply sarcastically, wrapping the scalpel in my hand in muslin before setting it in the sterilization tray. "You know. In a little while."

Becca leans back against the counter with a chuckle. "I thought you might say that." She taps a long fingernail on her arm thoughtfully. "So, Dr. Thompson might not be your Universe Guy, but he's still pretty cute, right?"

I roll my eyes. "If you and Jules think he's such hot stuff, you guys should go after him."

"Jules thinks he's hot?"

"What female in that room didn't?" I reply with a shrug. "He was hot even before he opened his mouth."

Becca sighs dreamily. "Yeah, that accent is pretty amazing." She shudders dramatically.

I wrap the last instrument and settle it in the tray, then slide the tray into the autoclave and switch it on. We both step back to let it do its thing.

"Look. I get it. He's my type. He's hot. He's British. But he's also a doctor, a coworker, and too old for me. I appreciate that you guys want me to find a guy, but I promise that I'm *happy* being single."

Becca looks past me, agape. On instinct, I turn around. And Dr. Caleb Thompson is standing in the doorway with a look on his face that says he heard everything. I internalize a heavy sigh. Yep. That's about right. That's pretty much how things go for me when it comes to men I might potentially be interested in.

"Is there something I can help you with, Dr. Thompson?" I ask as evenly as I can, but inside I'm dying. Becca skitters out of the room, just squeezing by him. The fucking traitor.

"I'm sorry, I — I didn't mean to interrupt anything, I'll just ... I can come back later ..." He's clearly horribly embarrassed, as he's stumbling over every other word.

Despite my best efforts, I feel the heat creep up my cheeks. "No, I'm sorry. We shouldn't have been —"

"It's okay, I really should ... I can come back later." He turns, but I stop him with a hand on his arm.

"Please, can we just pretend like that never happened?" I shift nervously from foot to foot as his gaze meets mine. His clear blue eyes search mine for a moment, and my stomach flip-flops.

"I'm sorry, pretend what never happened?" he replies with a small smile.

Some of the tension in my shoulders lift at his obvious out.

"You needed something?" I prompt, but still pretty much just wanting this to be over with so I can go crawl in a hole and die.

"Yes, of course," he replies, finding himself again. "I wanted to acquaint myself with the supplies, since I needed a few things anyway. I have a catheter angiography this afternoon."

"Well, I'm happy to show you where everything is, but one of us will take care of all of that for you," I assure him.

"I'm perfectly happy to, especially at first. It'll be good for me to get to know where things are and how everything works, just in case."

Ugh. Seriously? As if his mere presence doesn't reduce me to an idiotic mess, he's also willing to do menial work that most doctors, especially surgeons, see as a waste of their time. They almost always expect the nurses to take care of everything that doesn't strictly require an M.D. I mean, I get it, there are more nurses per patient than doctors, but still. He couldn't just be smart and gorgeous, he had to be considerate too. And against my better judgment, I want to know more about him.

"In that case, I'll give you the grand tour," I reply. I can only hope focusing on explaining everything will help me stay coherent this close to him. So I proceed to show him everything in the room, including a brief description of the sterilization process we use, before suggesting we go to the standard supply closet.

"Yes, excellent, let's," he replies, tapping a finger to the side of his jaw. "But just one quick thing."

I pause, looking up at him expectantly. "Yes?"

"For the record … I'm only thirty-two," he says, as a blush creeps up his neck.

I suck my lips into my mouth to stop myself from smiling, and my stomach does another little flip-flop. Breathe, Sasha, just breathe. He ducks his head self-consciously.

"Duly noted, Dr. Thompson," I reply, looking away to hide my blush.

He looks up sheepishly. "After you, then, Nurse Suvorin," he replies with a stern tone and a mock-serious expression to match.

I'm usually a hard nut to crack, but that does it, and I can't help laughing. I gesture for him to follow as I continue his tour.

Not long after, we part ways, as he's off to another consultation, this time with Dr. MacDougall. And Becca is waiting at the nurses' station, obviously bursting to know what happened.

"You're dead, Dillon," I say. "How could you leave me like that?"

She pushes up on the balls of her feet and wrings her hands together. "I know, I'm sorry. I panicked. But it looks like you did just fine." She gives me a pleading look, inviting me to spill every detail.

"Only because he's such a gentleman," I insist. "But I'm still humiliated. God, I can't believe he *heard* that." I swipe a hand over my eyes, not wanting to go full meltdown in case he happens by again. "We need to seriously can it with the personal talk at work."

"Aw, man. Does that mean you're not going to tell me more?" Becca pouts.

"Later," I insist, watching as one of my least favorite medical assistants, Lacey Petersen, heads towards us. Becca catches sight of her and nods understandingly.

"Gotcha. Drinks after work?"

"Dinner. You can drink if you want, but I'm going to need to eat. I've got a packed schedule this afternoon and I have to study later."

"Fine, fine," she agrees. She waits a moment for Lacey to drop off some paperwork and walk away. "But come on, just give me *one* detail before you go."

I'm not normally one for gossip. But remembering the sparkle in his eyes when he was looking down at me in the sterilization room has me hard-pressed to keep from smiling. I inhale and close my eyes, letting myself sink into that moment. Allowing myself just a bit of hope before I squirrel it all away inside, never again to see the light of day.

"He wanted me to know, for the record, that he's thirty-two."

Becca squeals as quietly as she can manage. "He likes you," she whispers gleefully.

"I think he was just trying to make me feel better. You wanted a detail, now you've got one. Don't make a thing of it." I shoot her a firm look before returning to my rounds. But as soon as my back is turned, the façade melts, and I allow myself my own gleeful grin. Though I almost immediately chastise myself for it. *No, Sasha. Strictly off limits.* And I keep repeating it in my head every time my thoughts drift where they shouldn't that afternoon. Eventually I lose track of how many times.

# ABOUT THE AUTHOR

Melanie A. Smith is an award-winning and international best-selling author of steamy contemporary romance fiction. Originally from upstate New York, she spent most of her childhood in the San Francisco Bay Area before moving to Los Angeles for college. After that, she spent almost fifteen years in the Seattle Area, and now lives in the Dallas-Fort Worth area of Texas with her family.

A voracious reader and lifelong writer, Melanie's writing began at a young age with short stories and poetry. Having completed a bachelor of science in electrical engineering at the University of California, Los Angeles, and a master's in business administration at the University of Washington, her writing abilities were mainly utilized for technical documents as a lead engineer for the Boeing Company, where she worked for ten years.

After shifting careers to domestic engineering and property management in 2015, she eventually found a balance where she was able to return to writing fiction.

Melanie is also a Mensan and enjoys spending time with her family, cooking, and driving with the windows down and the stereo cranked up loud.

# LINKS

For updates on my books, exclusives, giveaways, freebies, and more, sign up for my newsletter here: https://mailchi.mp/melanieasmithauthor/signup

For exclusive swag, updates, giveaways, ARCs, and more, sign up my street team here: https://mailchi.mp/melanieasmithauthor/romancereadersquad

Follow me on
Instagram: instagram.com/melanieasmithauthor
Facebook: http://fb.me/MelanieASmithAuthor
Twitter: https://twitter.com/MelASmithAuthor
Goodreads: https://www.goodreads.com/author/show/18088778.Melanie_A_Smith
BookBub: https://www.bookbub.com/profile/melanie-a-smith
Tumblr: http://melanieasmithauthor.tumblr.com/

# BOOKS BY MELANIE A. SMITH

## The Safeguarded Heart Series
The Safeguarded Heart
All of Me
Never Forget
Her Dirty Secret (audiobook also available on Audible and iTunes)
Recipes from the Heart: A Companion to the Safeguarded Heart Series
The Safeguarded Heart Complete Series: All Five Books Plus Exclusive Bonus Material

## Standalone Romance Novels
Everybody Lies
(audiobook also available on Audible and iTunes)
Last Kiss Under the Mistletoe (Coming December 2020)

## Life Lessons: A series that can be read as standalones
Never Date a Doctor
Bad Boys Don't Make Good Boyfriends
You Can't Buy Love

CPSIA information can be obtained
at www.ICGtesting.com
Printed in the USA
BVHW082250030820
585393BV00002B/45